a night's tail

a night's tail

A MAGICAL CATS MYSTERY

Sofie Kelly

BERKLEY PRIME CRIME
new york

BERKLEY PRIME CRIME
Published by Berkley
An imprint of Penguin Random House LLC
1745 Broadway, New York, NY 10019

Library of Congress Cataloging-in-Publication Data

Names: Kelly, Sofie, 1958– author.
Title: A night's tail: a magical cats mystery / Sofie Kelly.
Description: First edition. | New York: Berkley Prime Crime, 2019. |
Series: Magical cats; 11
Identifiers: LCCN 2019012522 | ISBN 9780440001133 (hardcover) |
ISBN 9780440001140 (ebook)
Subjects: | BISAC: FICTION / Mystery & Detective / Women Sleuths. |
GSAFD: Mystery fiction.
Classification: LCC PR9199.4.K453 N54 2019 | DDC 813/.6—dc23
LC record available at https://lccn.loc.gov/2019012522

First Edition: September 2019

Printed in Canada
1 3 5 7 9 10 8 6 4 2

Cover art by Tristian Elwell
Cover design by Rita Frangie
Book design by Kelly Lipovich

acknowledgments

Once again, thanks go to my editor, Jessica Wade, and her assistant, Miranda Hill, who work very hard to make me look good. Thank you as well to my agent, Kim Lionetti, who I definitely want on my team if there's a zombie apocalypse!

I am deeply grateful for the support and encouragement of my friends, both online and off, and for all my readers: Team Owen and Team Hercules.

And thanks always to Patrick and Lauren, who don't complain (much) when I wander around the house talking to people no one can see. Love you.

a night's tail

chapter 1

I turned my head when I caught sight of the bodies, but by then it was too late. I wasn't going to be able to forget what I had just seen—even after a brief glimpse. I shielded my face with one hand. "Please tell me that's not . . ."

"Sorry. It is," my best friend, Maggie, said in my ear.

I sighed because the last thing I'd wanted to see that night—or any other night, for that matter—was those two bodies: Mary Lowe, who worked with me at the library, and Sandra Godfrey, who was my mail carrier, both dancing on the T-shaped stage of The Brick in black satin and possibly peacock feathers. I wasn't taking a second look to find out for certain.

Mary was tiny and grandmotherly with fluffy gray hair and

a collection of cardigans for every season and holiday. That morning she'd been wearing one decorated with an unexpected combination of snowflakes and leprechauns, which was oddly appropriate for early March in Minnesota. The temperature hadn't gotten above freezing all day and there was a good five inches of new snow on the ground from a storm early in the week.

Mary may have looked like the stereotypical cookie-baking grandma—and she was—but she was also the state kickboxing champion in her age group, which was why every teenage boy who came into the library remembered to say "please" and "thank you" and never wore his baseball cap backward in her presence, at least never more than once.

Sandra Godfrey, on the other hand, was quiet and thoughtful, and almost half Mary's age. She was tall with great legs from all the walking she did on her mail route. She and Mary had struck up a friendship when Sandra had helped us with a collection of photos that had been found behind a wall at the post office and had ended up in the library's possession.

"You didn't tell me that they moved amateur night," I said to Maggie.

"I didn't know," she replied, somewhat absently. She was staring in the direction of the stage, a slight frown creasing her forehead, green eyes narrowed. "Do you have any idea where Mary got those peacock feathers?"

"No," I said. "She didn't mention them."

This wasn't the first time I'd accidentally stumbled across

Mary dancing. She had fabulous legs for a woman of any age and she didn't lack self-confidence. But it was hard—at least for me—to nonchalantly discuss library usage figures with someone I'd seen the night before doing a bump and grind to Meghan Trainor's "All About that Bass," especially since I knew that *someone* was likely to offer to loan me a bustier and fishnets so I could try getting up on stage myself. Mary had teasingly offered more than once to teach me some moves. I just couldn't picture myself dancing in front of what seemed like half of Mayville Heights in any kind of feathers—peacock or otherwise.

We were at The Brick, a club that featured exotic dancing, including a once-a-week amateur night, along with some surprisingly good local bands the rest of the time. It was dark and loud and smelled like beer and fries. My stomach growled.

I surveyed the crowded space and caught sight of my brother, Ethan, at a table on the other side of the room, gesturing with his hands as he talked, the way he'd been doing since he'd first learned to talk. Ethan was average height, four or five inches above my five foot six. We had the same dark hair but he wore his messy and spiky these days, while mine brushed my shoulders. He had hazel eyes where mine were brown, a rangy build and our mother's charm. The two of *us* actually looked more alike than either of us did to our sister, Sara, who was also Ethan's twin, but the two of *them* shared the same fiery intensity when they felt passionate about something, be it purple crayons, Vans shoes or food waste.

"Over there," I said to Maggie, tugging on the sleeve of her red-plaid jacket and gesturing toward the back wall with my free hand. I had worked late at the library and Maggie had had a meeting at the artists' co-op that she was part of, which was why we were late joining everyone.

"What? Oh, okay," she said, giving her head a shake and turning her attention back to me. I had a feeling she was still thinking about those peacock feathers. As an artist, Maggie could be pretty intense herself sometimes.

We were almost at the table when a man tapped Maggie on the shoulder. She turned around to see who it was.

"Zach, hi," she said, a smile lighting up her face.

"Hey, Mags, what are you doing here?" he asked. He had thick brown hair pulled back in a man bun and dark skin. He was wearing jeans and a snug-fitting black T-shirt from the Rolling Stones' Voodoo Lounge Tour. His most striking feature was his startlingly deep blue eyes.

"Meeting some friends," she said. "Are you working tonight?"

Zach nodded but he'd already turned his attention to me. "Hi, Maggie's friend," he said with a smile. "I'm Zach Redmond."

"Hi, Zach," I said. "I'm Kathleen." He was cute in a naughty-little-boy sort of way.

My stomach growled then. Loudly.

"Aww, didn't anyone feed you today?" he asked.

A NIGHT'S TAIL

"I kind of missed supper." It had been a busy Friday night at the library. It had been a busy Friday period.

"Spicy fries," he said, snapping his fingers. "Come up to the bar. I'll take care of you." He winked and gave me his naughty-boy smile again.

I smiled back at him. "I'll keep that in mind."

He lifted a hand in good-bye to Maggie and headed for the bar, weaving through the crowd.

Maggie had been watching our conversation with an amused expression on her face. "Zach is in my yoga class," she said. As well as being an artist Mags taught yoga and tai chi. Her tai chi class was where we'd first met. "He's also a big flirt."

I nodded. "It was hard not to notice that."

"He's like a big untrained puppy. Sometimes you have to smack him on the nose with a rolled-up newspaper."

I laughed at the mental picture of Maggie at the front of her yoga class with a rolled-up copy of the *Mayville Heights Chronicle* at her side.

Marcus got to his feet as we reached the table, giving me a smile that still made my stomach flutter. Detective Marcus Gordon was tall with wavy dark hair and blue eyes. What mattered was that he was a good man; ethical, hardworking, kind. I smiled, remembering how Mary had once described him: *"He is a good man inside, but that candy shell outside looks pretty dang delicious!"* I had to admit she was right.

Marcus looked around, spotted an empty chair and gestured to me to take his seat while he went to get the chair.

I sat down next to Brady Chapman as Maggie took the empty seat on the other side of him that he'd somehow managed to save for her. Brady was . . . I wasn't exactly sure what he was when it came to Maggie. They were more than friends but they weren't exactly a couple, either. I noted the way they smiled at each other and how their eyes stayed linked a little longer than just friends' would.

Brady had pale blue eyes and salt-and-pepper hair he wore clipped short. He liked science fiction—novels and movies—pinball and a good argument. He'd practiced law in Chicago but Mayville Heights had eventually called him back home, although he still took cases in Minneapolis, an hour away, from time to time. He was deep in conversation with Ethan at the moment, elbows propped on the table, which was cluttered with glasses and empty plates.

Ethan, along with the members of his band, The Flaming Gerbils, was going to be in Mayville Heights for the next two weeks with a three-night gig in Milwaukee scheduled for the middle of the visit. It would be the most time we'd spent together since I'd moved to Minnesota just over three years ago. The band had just finished a successful string of club dates in the Midwest—Chicago, Springfield, Des Moines, Kansas City and Minneapolis.

Ethan was spending time with me, his first visit since I'd moved to Minnesota or, as he liked to teasingly call it, the Land of Bigfoot and Lumberjacks. The rest of the band, Milo and Devon—Jake had left the group to go to art school—were taking a break and, in Milo's case, planning a visit to a woman in Red Wing who made guitars and restored vintage instruments. Devon had met a girl in an online chat room and gone to see her.

"He thinks she might be the one," Ethan had said when I'd asked where their bandmate was.

"Not again," I'd said, rolling my eyes. Devon fell in love more frequently than most people got their teeth cleaned.

Milo had shrugged. "The guy is a romantic. What else would you expect from a dude whose favorite movie is *The Princess Bride*?"

Milo was across the table from me now, leaning back in his chair, one hand tented over the beer in front of him and an amused smile on his face as Ethan continued his conversation with Brady, hands darting through the air. Milo, who was the Gerbils's bass player, looked like a young Timothy B. Schmit from the Eagles, dark hair halfway down his back, dark eyes, long fingers. He was hoping the luthier in Red Wing could restore a battered vintage Martin acoustic bass he'd bought for a few dollars in a yard sale at an old farmhouse in Maine.

Marcus had come back with the chair, which he squeezed in next to me. He sat down and I felt the warmth of his arm against mine. Derek Hanson was on his other side. He was The Flaming Gerbils's opening act and he'd been sitting in with the band on some of their songs, playing lead guitar on several of them since Jake was gone.

Ethan and the guys were in their early twenties while Derek, I was guessing, was in his late thirties. I knew he had one son, Liam, from a relationship he'd had when he was twenty. He'd told me in a voice edged with pride that his son was graduating in a couple of months and was headed for college in the fall. Derek had fair hair streaked with gray that looked like he'd missed a haircut, and a day or so of scruff on his face most of the time. He was a big man, solid and an inch or two taller than Marcus's six feet.

He touched my arm. "Kathleen, I'm going for a beer," he said. "Can I get you anything?"

My stomach gurgled again. It was hard not to be enticed by the smell of French fries. "A plate of spicy fries and a small ginger ale," I said, fishing in my pocket for my wallet.

Derek shook his head. "Don't worry about it," he said. "You've fed me three times in the last day. I can spring for a few fries."

"Uh, thanks," I said. Ethan was staying with me while the guys were at a bed-and-breakfast downtown. I'd volunteered to feed everyone.

This was the first time Derek had offered to pay for anything since the guys had gotten to town. Ethan had arrived with a box of chocolate mice from L.A. Burdick in Back Bay—one of my favorite treats. Milo had shown up with a couple of gallons of milk at breakfast—"I've seen Ethan eat cereal," he'd said with a grin as he stashed the containers in my refrigerator.

Derek gestured at the glass on the table in front of Marcus. "You want another one?"

"I'm driving," I added.

Marcus nodded. "Yeah, thanks."

Derek waved away his money. "I've got this," he said. "You got the last round." He headed for the crowded bar.

I was finding it a bit of a challenge to warm up to Derek. He shared very little about himself so it was hard to get to know him. Or maybe it was just that I missed Jake, who'd been hanging around my parents' house since he and Ethan had met in sixth grade. Jake, who filled every scrap of paper he got his hands on with sketches of whatever happened to catch his eye, was an open book, quick to smile, quick to step up and help out. Derek was more like a book with uncut pages, a reference I realized only another librarian would understand.

Marcus leaned in close to my ear. "How was your day?" he asked.

"I think the printer is truly ready for last rites this time," I said. "Susan tried to fix it but she didn't have any luck."

"I didn't know Susan knew how to do that," Marcus said. "I would have gotten her to look at my printer instead buying a new one."

I held up a finger. "Number one, your printer was so old the company no longer had any customer service manuals for it, and number two"—I added another finger—"Susan's way of fixing the printer is to give it a couple of whacks on one side and use one of her made-up swear words." Before he could say anything I raised an eyebrow. "Although to be fair that has always worked with the library's coffeemaker."

Marcus laughed. "I'll keep that in mind. You know how often someone breaks a coffeemaker at the station." He shifted in his seat. We had more chairs at the table than it was designed for. "So what exactly is a made-up swear word?"

"Apparently the twins had picked up a couple of not-so-polite words. She told them to be more creative." Susan's identical twin boys were definitely creative. They were also scary smart.

"And they came up with?" Marcus raised an eyebrow.

"Glass bowl," I said. "According to Susan, useful when you're stuck in traffic."

He nodded. "I like it."

"Son of a horse."

Marcus shook his head and smiled. "I think I know how they came up with that one. I helped Eric get his car out of a snowbank last month."

I smiled back at him. "According to Susan he's behind all of the boys' questionable vocabulary." Eric Cullen was the twins' father and Susan's husband. He also owned Eric's Place, my favorite place to eat in town.

Off to the side I suddenly heard the sound of a dog whimpering followed by raised voices. Marcus and I both turned in the direction of the noise. Two tables away, closer to the busy bar, was a man who looked to be in his early thirties with a service dog, a beautiful German shepherd with dark-chocolate-and-black coloring. The man had two prosthetic legs. A veteran, maybe? One arm was wrapped protectively around the dog. He was exchanging words with another man, who loomed over them.

The second man was just under six feet or so I was guessing—with a thick midsection, more fleshy than muscle. His brown hair was cut in a style that had taken a lot more than twenty minutes in a barber's chair. I was pretty sure his sweater was cashmere. His jeans were worn at both knees, but it was the kind of worn that he'd paid a lot of money for, not the result of a lot of hard days' labor. And he was drunk. I could see that his face was flushed and he swayed just a little. He wasn't standing up straight, I was guessing, because he wasn't capable of it.

Keith King was sitting at the same table and he got to his feet. Keith was on the library board and he was dad to Taylor, who had worked on our summer reading program. I couldn't catch all of what he said to the drunk but I could see the tension in his body, in his clenched fists and the rigid way he held his shoulders. The situation was close to getting out of hand. I couldn't get most of the drunken man's words but I could hear his tone and I didn't hear any remorse. He'd done something to the dog—kicked it most likely—that much was clear, and it didn't seem as though he was sorry.

Marcus had already gotten up and was making his way to the table with Brady right behind him. Before they could close the distance the drunk said something to Keith and I saw him pull back his leg, *like he was going to kick the dog* a second time.

He didn't get the chance. Derek was passing the table on his way up to the bar. His right fist caught the left side of the man's jaw. He swayed backward like an old-style inflatable clown punching bag. Marcus caught the man by the shirt collar just as one of the bouncers reached them. Derek gave his fist a shake like he was shaking off a cramp. I hadn't noticed him detour from his trek to the bar. Now he stood there glaring at the intoxicated man.

Everyone at the table had gotten to their feet with the exception of the man with the prosthetic legs. Keith and Derek were talking at the same time. The drunk was shouting and rubbing his chin. For a moment I thought I heard him say something about Christmas, which didn't make any sense. Marcus spoke to the bouncer, who nodded and then stood there, arms folded, black T-shirt stretched smooth over his muscles. Still holding on to the drunken man by the scuff of his neck, Marcus leaned down and spoke to the dog's owner. When he straightened up he said a few words to Derek before sending him back in our direction.

"You all right?" Ethan asked as Derek reached the table.

Derek nodded. "Asshole," he muttered darkly. The knuckles on his right hand were already starting to swell. Maggie pushed away from the table and headed to the bar without a word.

"Do you know that man?" I asked. "I thought I heard him say something about Christmas."

Derek flushed. "I think it was just a shot at my clothes." He glanced down at the red quilted vest and red-and-black shirt he was wearing. "Guy's a jerk."

I glanced around, wondering where the band we had come to hear was. People were restless, a lot of them on their feet, and too many voices just a bit too loud seemed to rumble through the room like distant thunder, warning that a storm might be ahead. Marcus may have diffused the immediate situation with Derek and the drunk, but that didn't mean that there still couldn't be trouble. People were looking our way. The drunk had looked familiar for some reason I couldn't place. I was guessing at least some people in the bar knew who he was.

I leaned across the table. "Sing something," I said to Ethan.

"Yeah right," he said, rolling his eyes. "I'll get the whole place doing 'Row, Row, Row Your Boat' as a round. Or would you rather we all held hands and sang 'Kumbaya'?"

I pushed my hair behind my ear with an impatient gesture. Ethan hated me telling him what to do. I had a mental image of him as a two-year-old, grabbing the socks I was trying to put on his chubby toddler feet, running down the hall and flinging them into the middle of the kitchen floor, standing there, feet planted wide apart, defiance blazing in his eyes.

I glared at him. "Don't act like a guy. I don't see any sign of the band or any more dancers. And it's getting tense in here."

He looked around. I knew he had to feel the unsettled energy in the room. "We don't have our instruments," he said, swiping a hand over his chin. I knew that gesture. He was thinking about what I'd said. "Anyway, we can't just start singing."

This time I rolled *my* eyes. "Right. Because you've never done *that* before."

Ethan made a face.

"'A Hundred Other Worlds,'" I said. "You don't need instruments for that song." "A Hundred Other Worlds" was my favorite Gerbils song. Ethan had written it. The love song featured just voices and guitar but it sounded equally beautiful with only the guys' perfect harmonies. "Please," I added.

He exhaled loudly. "I suppose next you'll play the 'I changed your diapers' card." The gleam in his eyes told me I'd already won.

I held up my phone. "No, but I could play the video of you drumming on a box of oatmeal, wearing nothing but a smile and a saggy diaper."

"You're mean," he said, but he was already getting up.

"*And* I'm older *and* I practice while you're asleep," I finished.

Ethan elbowed Milo and raised an eyebrow at Derek, tipping his head in the direction of the stage. Derek nodded and set the makeshift ice pack that Maggie had gotten for him—ice wrapped in a striped cotton bar towel—on the table.

"Thank you," I said.

Ethan shrugged. "Yeah, well if we don't sing the only other option would be you dancing."

I tried to swat him but he darted out of my way.

The three of them made their way over to the small stage the various bands used. Milo and Derek lined up behind Ethan, hands behind their backs. Ethan glanced over his shoulder at them, then turned to face the crowd and started to sing. He didn't have a mic. He didn't need one.

It started with the tables closest to the stage. People stopped what they were doing to listen, dropping back into their seats one after another, focused on the music, focused on Ethan's voice, on all three of their voices.

It gave me goose bumps. On the other side of the table Maggie was mesmerized. I saw her rub her hand over her arm as though maybe she had goose bumps, too.

A hand touched my shoulder. Marcus dropped into the chair beside me as Brady slid in next to Maggie. I linked my fingers with his but I couldn't take my eyes off of my baby brother. Neither could anyone else.

I'd always known Ethan had talent. He was three when, after standing for the national anthem at a Red Sox game, his tiny hand over his heart, he'd turned to Dad and proclaimed emphatically, "Out tune!" about the off-key actress who'd been singing. And he'd been right. It made my big-sister heart swell with pride to look around and see so many other people recognizing Ethan's talent.

They finished the song and for a few seconds silence hung in the air. Then someone began to clap. Someone else let out a long, sharp whistle. The crowd, as they say, went wild.

The scheduled band, the band we'd gone to The Brick to hear, showed up right after that. The Flaming Gerbils ended up sitting in for two songs with them. Someone found a guitar for Derek and once the crowd heard him play everyone seemed to forget about the earlier incident. He was good, I realized. Not Jake, but equally as talented. I leaned back against Marcus's shoulder, enjoying the music and the company, relieved that everything was okay.

Derek came back to the table when they finished and sank onto the chair next to me. Brady and Maggie were up dancing. "Kathleen, I'm sorry," he said, swiping a hand across his chin.

"You don't owe me an apology," I said.

"Yeah, I know," he said. "But these are your friends and people you know and work with and that guy acted like an ass."

I wasn't sure what he was getting at. I glanced over at the table where Keith King, the man and his service dog and their friends were still sitting. "He kicked the dog, didn't he?" I asked. "The drunk, I mean. And he was drunk."

Derek nodded. "Yeah, he kicked the dog—he was going to do it again—and he was drunk. Then he said something about freakin' animals being everywhere because guys have lost their . . ." He gestured with one hand and I was pretty sure I could guess how to finish the sentence. "I lost my cool. The guy's a vet. I saw his cap on the table. How could anyone say that about a man who's a hero and then kick his dog?"

"Your intentions were good," Marcus said, "but maybe next time you could let the dog's owner speak for himself first."

Derek nodded, but I saw a flash of annoyance in his eyes. "Right, I get it," he said. "It's just that my dad's a vet—Vietnam—and I walk dogs at a shelter back in Boston. I don't think that that kind of behavior should be ignored. I think it should be called out." There was a slight self-righteous edge to his voice.

Derek looked at Marcus. "I suppose there's going to be some kind of fine."

"No one was arrested," Marcus said. "No charges. No fines." I saw him glance at Brady. "The gentleman saw the error of his ways."

I wondered what Marcus and Brady had said to the man. I glanced over at the nearby table again. Keith caught my eye, raised one hand and smiled. I smiled back at him then I turned my attention to Derek again. "Do you have any idea who that man was?" I asked.

"He doesn't live around here?" Derek asked.

I shook my head. "No. But there was something familiar about him. It could just be that he's a tourist who came into the library looking for directions." Had the man been in the library? No, I was fairly certain I hadn't seen him there. Maybe I'd noticed him at Eric's Place when I was getting coffee. Or could he have been in the artists' co-op store when I stopped in to talk to Maggie?

"His name is Lewis Wallace," Marcus said.

I narrowed my eyes at him. "Wait a minute. The businessman that the development committee has been talking to? The one who might set up his new supplement business in one of the empty warehouses down by the waterfront?"

Marcus nodded.

Now I knew why I'd thought I'd seen Wallace somewhere before. Maggie and I had gone to a meeting about his pitch to the town. He hadn't been there, but there had been a photo of the man inside the information packet we'd received.

"Way to make a good impression," Derek said with an off-hand shrug.

Ethan came back to the table then, dropped into the chair across from me and grinned. "That was cool," he said, his face flushed, eyes gleaming. "Man, those guys are good." He looked at Derek. "That guitar is a Takamine?" It wasn't really a question.

Derek leaned an elbow on the table and smiled. "It is. I did like the way it sounds."

Ethan laughed. "So do I see one in your future?"

Derek shook his head. "Liam starts college in the fall, re-member?" He glanced at Marcus and me. "I never went to college. Not gonna happen to my kid. So no new guitars for his old man until he makes it big. My old Gibson is good enough for me."

Derek was a good enough musician that I felt certain he could have gotten music out of half a dozen rubber bands stretched over an empty cereal box. Ethan was watching me, I realized then, sprawled in his chair, a grin on his face.

"What?" I asked.

"Just waiting for you to say 'I told you so.' You're getting slow in your old age, big sister."

"I figured the 'I told you so' was self-evident." I leaned back in my own seat, copying his body language.

Ethan laughed. "This calls for a beer," he said.

The words were barely out of his mouth when our waiter appeared at the table with two pitchers of beer and a big basket heaped with spicy crispy fries.

"Thank you," I said to Marcus. He must have stopped at the bar on his way back to the table. My fries and the drinks had been forgotten in the aftermath of Derek's altercation with the drunken man.

"I didn't order anything," he said.

"I'm sorry. We didn't order any of that," I said to the waiter.

"This is from Mr. King," he said as he set the two pitchers in the center of the table. He put the fries in front of me. I glanced over at the bar. Zach, Maggie's bartender friend, lifted a hand in acknowledgment and smiled as though he'd been the one to send the fries and not Keith.

I snagged one French fry. They were crispy, hot and perfectly spiced. I could feel the heat on my tongue. I leaned sideways, caught Keith's attention and mouthed a thank-you. That got me a warm smile in return. Keith wasn't a demonstrative man. I realized the man with the service dog must be someone special to him.

Marcus and I got up to dance after I finished my basket of fries. He caught my hand and pulled me against him.

"Hey, this isn't one of those middle school clinch songs," I said, looking up into his gorgeous blue eyes. The band was doing their version of Bon Jovi's "Livin on a Prayer." I could see Maggie dancing with abandon, arms high over her head.

"Number one, I don't care," Marcus said, his warm breath tickling my hair. "Number two, what is a 'middle school clinch song'?"

"One of those slow songs they'd play at school dances back in seventh grade. The girl would put her head on the guy's shoulder and basically they'd just sway back and forth to the music."

"I never did that."

I tipped my head back to look at him. "Seriously?"

"Seriously," he said. "In seventh grade I still hadn't had my growth spurt and my mom cut my hair—bowl bangs. There wasn't one girl in the seventh grade who would have gotten this close to me back then."

I stood on tiptoe and kissed him. "Their loss," I said. It was hard to imagine a short version of Marcus with hair that looked like his mother had stuck a dish on his head to cut it. This Marcus had a smile that made women take a second look, and an honest-to-goodness six-pack.

Since it seemed we were going to keep dancing this close, I decided to just enjoy the warmth of his hand against my back and the way he smelled like citrusy aftershave and Juicy Fruit gum.

"Thank you for handling that drunk," I said. "What did you and Brady say to him?"

"I pointed out that I could arrest him for public intoxication and Brady added that I could add a charge for animal cruelty. He wasn't so drunk that he couldn't see if things went badly for Derek they'd also go badly for him."

"Did he know you recognized him?" I asked. "I can't help thinking that it doesn't exactly make his case for the town to give him a deal on that piece of property down on the waterfront if he's going around getting drunk and kicking service dogs."

Marcus shrugged. "I don't know. I asked him his name and he just laughed. Brady is the one who recognized him. I didn't want to escalate things by pushing for his ID. He probably thought it was funny that he was able to get away with acting like an idiot. And to be fair, maybe he was just having an off night. It happens."

He pulled me a little closer. "You know, I think I would have liked middle school clinch songs if you'd been at my middle school."

"I would have danced with you," I said.

"Even with my quasi–Tom Petty haircut?"

"That was the look you were going for?"

He reached over and tucked a stray strand of my hair behind my ear. "I was. I'm not really sure my mother even knew who Tom Petty was."

"Even if you'd had a haircut like Richard Petty the race-car driver I would have danced with you," I said.

He raised an eyebrow and a slow smile spread across his face. "For future reference, flattery works on me."

I gave his hand a squeeze. "Good to know," I said.

Off to my right I could see Maggie dancing with Brady. To my left the boys were still around the table, talking. I could almost see the energy radiating from Ethan, one hand wrapped around his beer, the other punctuating his sentences with sharp movements slicing through the air. He was like our mom. Performing energized them both.

We stayed for the band's second set and then headed home. Brady offered to drop off Milo and Derek at the bed-and-breakfast where they were staying but it was a nice night—clear and just a couple of degrees below freezing and they decided to walk down. Marcus, Ethan and I squeezed into the front seat of my truck.

"Is there going to be kissing?" Ethan asked, when I pulled in the driveway at Marcus's house. He squished his face and pulled his shoulders up around his ears. He was sitting in the middle between Marcus and me.

"Yes, there's going to be kissing." I leaned across him, covering his eyes with one hand, and gave Marcus a quick kiss.

"I'll call you after practice," he said.

Marcus was helping coach the girls' high school hockey team. They were just one win away from making it to the state finals.

I nodded.

"Good to see you, Ethan," he added and climbed out of the truck.

"Is it safe to look?" Ethan asked. I'd already dropped my hand. He opened one eye, squinting at me. "I don't want to see anything that might scar my psyche. I'm very sensitive."

"You're very something," I said. I straightened up and put the truck in gear.

Ethan slugged my shoulder with a loose fist and laughed. "C'mon, Kathleen, you know you've missed me."

"Like a root canal," I countered as I backed out of the driveway. "Like fingernails on a chalkboard." We'd been doing this routine for years.

"Do they still have chalkboards?" Ethan asked.

"Like a colonoscopy. Like Mom's hot cross buns." Our mother's hot cross buns were legendary. They looked like they belonged in an issue of *Bon Appétit*. But they were harder than a concrete paver. Dad had literally chipped a tooth on one of them, although as far as Mom was concerned the tooth had a weak spot and the fact that it broke when he took a bite of—or at least tried to take a bite of—one of her hot cross buns was just an unfortunate coincidence.

Ethan narrowed his eyes at me. "Ooooh, Mom's hot cross buns. Burn."

I glanced over at him, head back against the seat, fingers tapping a rhythm on his leg that only he could hear, and I was hit with a wash of homesickness, like someone had just upended a bucket of water over my head. I missed them: Mom, Dad, Sara and Ethan, even though he was right here beside me.

It wasn't easy being so far away from Boston, from all of them. Not that my family were always in Boston. Ethan was on the road a lot with the band. Sara's work as a makeup artist and filmmaker had her traveling more and more, and while Mom and Dad were teaching, they still went where the acting jobs were, which in my mother's case meant Los Angles a couple of times a year for a recurring role on the daytime drama *The Wild and Wonderful*.

On the other hand I had a life now in Minnesota, a life with Owen and Hercules, my cats, with Marcus and Maggie and a group of friends I'd miss just as much as I missed my family now, if I went back to Boston.

"Hey, I never did ask," Ethan began. "Did you know that dipwad in the bar?"

I shook my head. "No, I don't know him, at least not personally. He's here in Mayville Heights to maybe start a business."

"You get some interesting people in bars," Ethan said. "When we played in Chicago this woman got up on her chair, whipped off her shirt and started dancing. Then she yelled at me to come give her an autograph."

"I think that makes you a certified rock star," I teased, "being asked to autograph a woman's bra."

Ethan raised an eyebrow just the way I sometimes did, à la

Mr. Spock from *Star Trek*. "I didn't say she had a bra on under her shirt."

"Ewww," I said with a shudder. "Now *my* delicate psyche is scarred."

Ethan shook with laughter. "She was wearing a tank top. And I signed the *back* of it!" He spent the rest of the drive home sharing all the weird things he'd been asked to autograph, including a bald guy's head and the top of a toilet tank. I laughed so much I got hiccups and I forgot all about drunks in bars.

chapter 2

When I left for the library in the morning Ethan was at the table eating an omelet stuffed with ham and cheese, not even trying to disguise the fact that he was feeding bites to the two mooching furballs sitting at his feet.

"C'mon, try to pretend you're not sneaking them food," I said as I put on my shoes. "The least you could do is try to give me plausible deniability when Roma asks what they've been eating."

To my amusement Hercules immediately moved around to the far side of Ethan's chair so he was not so much in my direct line of sight. Ethan then made an elaborate show of "sneaking" a bite of ham to the cat, which was, of course, way more obvious than what he had been doing.

I checked my messenger bag to make sure I had all the papers I needed.

"So what's your friend Roma's problem with Owen and Hercules having a bit of egg once in a while?" Ethan asked.

Owen immediately gave a loud and somewhat indignant meow.

I rolled my eyes at the cat. "The problem is that it never stops at just a bit of egg once in a while. It starts there and all of a sudden it's an entire slice of pizza." Owen immediately licked his whiskers and Hercules leaned around the chair looking like he suddenly expected a fully loaded slice to materialize on a plate next to him on the floor.

"So please don't feed them any more people food," I continued. Owen meowed again. "Because no matter how much he may try to convince you otherwise, Owen is a cat."

Ethan looked down at the little gray tabby. "Sorry, dude, the boss has spoken."

Owen narrowed his golden eyes and his ears twitched. "I know," Ethan said, a conspiratorial edge to his voice. "She's been on me about my diet my entire life."

Ethan got a kick out of how the cats responded when he talked to them. Part of that was that I talked to them all the time. They were used to having to hold up their end of a conversation even if it was just by tipping their furry heads to one side and making occasional sounds that seemed to indicate that they were listening. And part of it was that Owen and Hercules *weren't exactly ordinary cats.* That was something I kept very much to myself.

Aside from the fact that they had been feral when I found them and didn't handle people other than me touching them very well, the boys had certain skills that regular cats didn't have. Owen could become invisible at will. It had seemed so shocking the first time I'd realized what he could do, and now it was no big deal—for the most part. Hercules, on the other hand—or maybe that should be "paw"—could walk through walls. Any kind of walls, from brick to wood to solid steel. They were no kind of obstruction to the little tuxedo cat. When Hercules had walked directly through a heavy, solid door into a meeting room at the library I wasn't sure if I was hallucinating or having some kind of breakdown.

I also had the feeling that both Owen and Hercules understood a lot more of what was said to them than probably even I knew. Given their other talents, it didn't seem that farfetched. Luckily for me, my friends were all cat people. No one thought me talking to the boys was the slightest bit odd. Owen adored Maggie, who returned his affection by keeping him in yellow catnip chickens. Hercules had befriended both Rebecca and Everett, who were our backyard neighbors. And both cats had formed a bond with my friend Ruby, an artist and photographer who had taken a series of photographs of the two of them for what had turned out to be a very successful promotional calendar for the town. The one person they were somewhat iffy about was Roma. She was the town veterinarian, so not only was she always reprimanding anyone who fed them people food, she was also the person who administered their shots.

"I'm leaving," I said to the room in general. "Are we still on for lunch?"

Ethan nodded over the top of his coffee cup.

"Okay, I'll see you at Eric's." I mock-glared at all three of them. "Try to stay out of trouble." All of them gave me their best innocent looks. I was not fooled.

Mountain Road, where my little white farmhouse was, curved in toward the center of town, so as I drove down the hill the roof of the library building came into view. The two-story brick building, which had originally been built in 1912, sat near the midpoint of a curve of shoreline and was protected from the water by a sturdy rock wall. The library featured an original stained-glass window at one end and a copper-roofed cupola, complete with the restored wrought-iron weather vane that had been attached to the roof when the library had been completed more than a century ago.

The Mayville Heights Free Public Library, like many others of its vintage, was a Carnegie library, built with funds donated by Scottish-American industrialist Andrew Carnegie. Everett Henderson had funded the renovations to the building, his gift to the town for the library's centennial, and had hired me to oversee everything as head librarian. In eighteen months I'd fallen in love with the town and the people, and when Everett and the library board had offered me a permanent job I'd said yes.

Abigail Pierce was just walking along the sidewalk as I pulled into the parking lot at the library. She waited for me at the front steps and smiled as I reached her. "How was The Brick?" she asked.

I studied her face for a moment then narrowed my gaze. "You knew," I said. Mary and Abigail were friends as well as co-workers. What were the chances Mary hadn't said what she was going to be doing last night? It was her day off, otherwise I knew she could easily have shown up with an oversized feather fan and an offer—again—to teach me how to dance.

Abigail cocked her head to one side. Her copper-red hair was streaked with silver and she wore it in a sleek, chin-length bob that showed off her beautiful cheekbones and blue eyes. Not only did she work at the library, she was also a very talented children's book author.

"I'm sorry, Kathleen, I don't know what you're talking about," she said. "Was there a problem of some kind last night?"

"Oh, no," I said as I started up the stairs. "The band was fantastic. Ethan and the guys did three songs as well."

Abigail's lips twitched but she managed to keep a straight face. "What kind of music?" she asked. "Did they play anything you could dance to?" She put a little extra emphasis on the word "dance."

I stared at her without speaking and she couldn't contain

her laughter any longer. "I swear I didn't know Mary was going to be dancing until after the library had closed and you were gone." She put up one hand as if to quell any objection I might make.

I opened the main doors, shut off the alarm and stepped into the library proper, marveling as I always did at the beauty of the restored building. A detailed mosaic floor was under our feet and all around the bright, open space was gorgeous wooden molding that had been meticulously refinished or carefully re-created to match the original.

"Mary and Sandra," I said, flipping on the lights.

"Wait a minute. Sandra Godfrey?" Abigail was already halfway to the stairs. She stopped and looked back over her shoulder at me.

I nodded. "I think there were peacock feathers involved."

"Sandra Godfrey dancing at amateur night at The Brick," Abigail said. "Mary had to have had a hand in that."

"From the very brief glimpse I got, Mary had more than just a hand in what was happening on that stage," I said.

That made Abigail laugh again. "Great. Now how am I supposed to get the image of Sandra wearing peacock feathers and very little else out of my head the next time she comes in to borrow some books?"

"You know, I admire their confidence, getting up and dancing like that," I said as we headed upstairs to the staff room. "I couldn't do that."

"That's because you can't dance," Abigail said.

She was right. I couldn't dance, I had no natural rhythm and it didn't matter how many containers you gave me—buckets or otherwise—I couldn't carry a tune. "Everyone else in my family can sing and dance, you know. For a while when I was a teenager I thought I'd been left by gypsies."

"Gypsies who loved books and loved to organize things," Abigail finished.

I grinned at her. "Pretty much."

She pointed over her shoulder at her backpack. "I have muffins," she said, waggling her eyebrows at me, "from Sweet Thing."

Sweet Thing, a small bakery run by Georgia Tepper, was best known for its cupcakes, but Georgia had recently started making muffins as well.

"The way to my heart," I said, putting both hands on the left side of my chest.

Abigail laughed. "I thought coffee was the way to your heart."

I nodded. "It is. Oh, and pizza and Eric's chocolate pudding cake." I was still listing my favorite things to eat as we reached the staff room.

Abigail made the coffee while I dropped my things in my office. Then we took a few minutes to go over our plans for the upcoming Money Week we had planned for mid-April. We were going to talk about taxes, budgets and debt. We had several speakers scheduled, including a woman who ran a popular frugal-living blog. There were workshops planned for adults and teens. A couple of teachers at the high school were bringing their classes to the talk about budgets. Before that, in a little less than three weeks, we were going to be home to the Mayville Heights quilt festival, along with the St. James Hotel.

Abigail turned on our computers and started on the contents of the book drop. I went to my office to call Harrison Taylor. Harrison was in his early eighties and the first time I'd seen him—in a chair in my backyard—I'd thought I was looking at Santa Claus. He had thick white hair and a snowy beard. There was generally a twinkle in his eye as well.

Harrison was a wellspring of information about Mayville Heights and the surrounding area. He'd done one well-received talk about the history of the town and due to popular demand—and the fact that he'd lost a wager about attendance at the first talk—he was going to do a second.

"You set me up, Kathleen," he said. I knew from the tone of his voice that he wasn't really annoyed that I'd won our bet. Harrison was charming, well-spoken and an excellent public speaker. His talk had been standing-room only, just as I'd expected, which is why I'd made the wager in the first place. We'd been sitting in Fern's Diner when I'd first made my proposition. It hadn't been hard to talk him into saying yes.

"You come and talk for about half an hour about the history of the town—time period to be determined—and then you answer questions. If my meeting room isn't full I'll treat you to the biggest steak Peggy has out back," I'd said, tipping my head in the direction of the diner's kitchen.

"Like shooting fish in a barrel," I told him now. "Would you like to hazard a guess about how many people are going to show up this time?"

His laughter boomed through the phone. "Not likely. I may have been born at night, young lady, but it wasn't last night."

It was a busy morning at the library. The sunshine seemed to bring out more people than usual, that and the fact that several teachers at the high school had assigned papers due in the next two weeks. When we closed for the day at lunchtime I headed over to Eric's Place to meet Ethan and Derek for lunch.

I decided to leave my truck in the lot and walk over. The streets in Mayville Heights that ran from one end of town to the other all followed the curve of the shoreline, so it was a short walk to the café. The snow that had fallen earlier in the week was already melting and the sidewalks were dry and bare for the most part. Winter in Mayville Heights, Minnesota, came in three varieties: About to Snow, Snowing and Get Out the Shovel, and by March we were all grateful for a sunny day with the temperature above freezing.

As I headed down the sidewalk toward the café I caught sight of Derek standing nose to nose with Lewis Wallace, the drunk from the night before. My stomach sank. I could see belligerence in the businessman's stance. I remembered the arrogance I'd noted in his body language and demeanor the night before and realized I'd been unrealistic to think the problem had passed.

I started walking faster but before I got to them Ethan stepped between the two men, pushing Derek back, one hand shoving hard against his chest. At the same time he said something to Wallace, pointing down the sidewalk with his other hand. Wallace made one last comment to the two of them that I couldn't hear before he walked away, making a dismissive gesture with one hand. He got into a Big Bird–yellow Hummer wedged in at the curb and drove off.

As I reached them Derek pushed Ethan's arm away and took a couple of steps back, holding one hand in the air like a warning. His face was flushed and he raked a hand back through his hair the way Marcus did when something was bothering him.

Ethan was trying to say something to his friend. Bad idea, I knew. I caught his arm and he turned, just seeming to realize that I was there. "Give him a minute," I said. Derek had turned away from us and I knew the best thing to do was let him be while he got his anger under control.

Anger flashed in Ethan's hazel eyes. "I'm not six, Kathleen," he snapped. He shook off my hand.

I took a breath and let it out. "I know that. I just want to know what's going on because I need to know if this is something Marcus should hear about." I lowered my voice slightly. "He didn't make an issue out of what happened last night, which let that guy off the hook, but don't forget he's not the only one who got to walk away."

Ethan folded one arm over the top of his head, his fingers digging into the bottom of his skull. "I'm sorry. We were just coming out of that bookstore. The dipwad from last night had right then parked his big-ass vehicle and gotten out. When he saw Derek he came across the sidewalk and got in his face almost like they knew each other or something. What a jerk!"

"Yeah, he is," Derek said behind us.

I turned to look at him. The angry flush had faded from his cheeks.

"He's a first-class jerk. Forget about him. I don't want to waste one more bit of air on that guy. C'mon, I'm hungry. Let's have lunch." He looked at Ethan. "And I sort of have this idea for a song that's been rolling around my head all morning." His gaze shifted to me. "I'm good. I swear."

Ethan bumped me with his hip as we started for the door. "A word of warning. Derek is about to fall down a rabbit hole."

"I am not," Derek retorted.

Ethan just looked at his friend, a smile playing around his mouth.

"Okay, so maybe I can get a little distracted when I'm working on a song."

"A little?" Ethan snorted.

We stepped inside the café and Claire came around the counter with a smile. She carried three menus and, because she knew me well, the coffeepot.

Ethan immediately stood up straighter and smiled. Talk about getting distracted.

"Hi, Kathleen," Claire said. Her red curls were pulled up in two pigtails and she was wearing her dark-framed glasses instead of contacts. "Would you like that table by the window?" She gestured at one of my favorite places to sit in the small restaurant. I could see all the way to the water out of the front window.

"Please," Ethan said. "I mean, if it's not too much trouble. We can sit closer to the counter if that would be easier for you." Like Mom, he was a bit of a flirt.

"Claire, this is my brother, Ethan, and our friend Derek," I said.

She smiled at Ethan then turned to Derek. "You were in yesterday for lunch."

"You recommended that noodle bowl," he said. "It was pretty good."

"That does sound good," I said as we headed toward our table. I took the chair closest to the window. Ethan sat next to me and Derek took a seat across from us.

Claire handed us menus, then reached for the heavy stoneware mug in front of me and poured a cup of coffee. "How about you two?" she asked, looking from Derek to Ethan.

Both men nodded.

"Do you need some time with the menu?" she asked after she'd filled the guys' cups.

"I don't," I said. "I think I'll have the ramen bowl."

"Me too," Derek said. He'd only given the menu a quick glance.

"I'm game," Ethan said. "Unless there's something else you'd recommend."

I fought the urge to roll my eyes.

"I think you'll like the ramen bowl," Claire said. She shot me a quick bemused glance. I was pretty sure she already had Ethan's number.

"It won't be long," she added. She collected our menus and headed for the kitchen.

I added cream and sugar to my coffee and then focused my attention on Derek. I really did want to get to know him better. "Derek, do you mind telling me a little about how you write a song?" I asked. "Which comes first? The words or the music?"

"Well, that depends," he said, propping his elbows on the table. "A lot of times a few words or a sentence come to me and the song starts from there. Other times it's a few notes of music."

"How long does it take?"

He shrugged. "Again, that depends. I've written songs in less than a day and there are some that took weeks."

Ethan pointed a finger at Derek. "'Begin Again,'" both men said at the same time.

"We wrote that song together," Derek explained, seeing my confused expression. "We were stuck on one line—one line— for I don't know, three weeks maybe. It drove me crazy."

Ethan cleared his throat.

Derek turned his head. "Are you hacking up something or was that commentary?"

Ethan was turned sideways in his chair, one hand wrapped around his coffee mug. "Drove you crazy?" he said. "*You* drove everyone around you crazy." He gestured with his free hand. "I'm not kidding, Kath. One of his neighbors called the police for a wellness check because she was worried that Derek was suffering from some kind of mental health crisis because he was wandering around the block talking to himself!"

Derek laughed, a bit shame-faced. "Okay, I admit that I can get a bit of tunnel vision when I'm stuck on a song."

Ethan leaned his head in my direction, a conspiratorial tone to his voice. "Same woman who called the police for the wellness check? She made him a fanny pack with change for the T, some wet wipes and a baggie of granola in case he wandered too far away and got hungry."

"Don't knock it," Derek said with a grin. "That was homemade granola that Mrs. Melanson made herself with a bunch of that dried fruit and chocolate chips. It was really good."

Claire arrived then with our steaming ramen bowls. We ate, we laughed, we talked about song writing and the tour and life in general and I thought how happy I was to be spending time with my brother. I noticed Derek glance out the window a couple of times and I hoped that Lewis Wallace left town soon.

After lunch—which Ethan insisted on paying for—the guys decided to head to the co-op store. Maggie had mentioned some guitar straps that Ethan wanted to see.

"Would you give this to Maggie, please?" I asked, taking a small brown paper bag out of my bag.

"Sure," Ethan said. "What is it?"

"It's a peanut butter and banana muffin—her favorite—from Sweet Thing."

He frowned. "Sweet Thing?"

"It's a bakery. She'll know," I said. I'd swiped it from the box Abigail had brought in—with her permission.

I walked back to the library to get the truck because I had to go over to Fern's Diner to drop off a large coffeemaker that Peggy had loaned me for Harrison Taylor's talk about Mayville Heights's history. The library's coffeemaker had died, shooting water and coffee all over the staff room in one messy last hurrah.

Eight or nine years ago, Fern's had been restored to its 1950s glory, or as Roma liked to describe it, "Just like the good old days only better." The building was low and long, with windows on three sides, aglow with neon after dark. Inside there was the all-important jukebox, booths with red vinyl seats and a counter with gleaming chrome stools. The diner's claim to fame was Meatloaf Tuesday: meatloaf, mashed potatoes, green beans in the summer, carrots the rest of the time, brown gravy and apple pie.

It was quiet at Fern's. Larry Taylor was in the back corner at a table by himself, having a late lunch. Larry was Harrison's younger son, an electrician who had done a lot of work at the library. He raised a hand in hello and I waved back at him.

"You didn't have to rush to bring this back," Peggy said. She was wearing polka-dot pedal pushers, a short-sleeved white shirt with *Peggy Sue* stitched over the left breast pocket and rhinestone-tipped, cat's-eye-framed glasses. Her hair was in a bouffant updo with a red bow bobby-pinned at the front.

"Thanks for lending it to us on short notice," I said, laying a hand on the top of the box that held the coffeemaker. "I ordered a new one and it should be here on Monday."

Peggy took the box and set it behind the counter. "Well, if you need it again, just let me know."

Peggy had been seeing Harrison Taylor for months now, or as he liked to describe it, "keeping company." Since I regularly spent time with the old man, I'd gotten to know her better. Although Peggy was a lot younger than Harrison, she'd been good for him, getting him to keep doctors' appointments and cut back on caffeine. Most of all, he was happy, which was all any of us cared about.

Behind me the door to the diner opened and Georgia Tepper came in, carrying a large cardboard box with the logo of her company, Sweet Thing, stamped on top. Her shoulders were hunched, body rigid, and she was clenching her teeth. When I saw who was behind her I understood why.

"No," I said, under my breath. It was Lewis Wallace yet again. Why on earth was he turning up all over town?

He was hitting on Georgia, that much was obvious. He towered over her; in fact, he seemed to take up way too much space in the diner, and way too much air. "I'd love a little taste of something sweet," he was saying.

My first impression of Wallace hadn't been a good one and neither had the second and now the third. The man used his size to bully people and his lack of self-awareness was disturbing. He put a hand on Georgia's shoulder and she stiffened, twisting her body out of his grasp as she moved sideways.

Wallace looked at the box she was holding. "Aww, don't be like that, sweet thing," he said as he reached over and trailed a finger down the arm of her jacket.

Out of the corner of my eye I saw Larry stand up. At the same time Peggy and I both began to move toward Georgia. She stepped sideways again, closer to Lewis Wallace, coming down hard on his left foot in his not-appropriate-for-March-in-Minnesota Italian leather loafers with the chunky heel of her boot.

"Hey, watch it!" he exclaimed, grimacing and taking a step backward.

Georgia was trembling, almost imperceptibly, but her voice was steady when she said, "You should really watch where you put your . . . feet."

"Is everything all right?" I said, walking over to her.

Georgia nodded. "Yes, it is."

Wallace shook his head and said, "Jeez, a guy can't even give a girl a compliment anymore." He looked at Larry, who had just joined us. "Am I right?"

"No," Larry said. "You're not." Larry was one of the most easy-going people I knew. He, too, was a big man. Unlike

Wallace with his doughy build, Larry was all solid muscle, with blond hair and green eyes. I'd never thought of him as being the slightest bit intimidating. Until now.

Wallace looked at us for a long moment. "Aww, screw it," he said. He turned and went back out the door.

I took the big box of cupcakes from Georgia and handed it to Peggy. "Are you okay?" I asked.

She nodded. "I am. Thank you." She looked at Larry. "Thank you, too."

"Georgia, do you know Larry?" I said.

The question got a tiny smile out of her. "I've seen you around town," she said, directing that small smile at him.

He nodded. "I've had a couple . . . dozen of your cupcakes." He patted his stomach.

Georgia glanced at the door. "That guy is creepy. He followed me across the parking lot and he wouldn't stop hitting on me."

Larry shrugged. "Yeah, well, he has that reputation."

"So you know him?" Georgia asked.

"I know of him," Larry said. "His name is Lewis Wallace."

Peggy was nodding. "I thought that was him. He's the one the development committee is talking to. They're hoping he'll set up his new business in one of the empty warehouses down by the waterfront, if he gets everything he wants."

I remembered the information packet I'd brought home from the meeting Maggie and I had attended. "Wallace is a former athlete, isn't he?" I said. "Football?"

Larry nodded. "He played college ball but he couldn't cut it in the NFL. He wasn't really big enough. So he went to Canada and played there for a few years. Offensive lineman."

"Offensive *hu*man from what I saw," Peggy said drily.

Georgia's hand was still trembling. She stuffed it in the pocket of her jacket. Given her past experiences, including her connection to the death of businessman Mike Glazer, it was no wonder she was shaky.

It wasn't the only reason confrontations made her uneasy. Georgia had changed her name when she'd come to Mayville Heights. Before that she had been Paige Wyler. Her in-laws hadn't liked her from the moment she'd married their son. He'd died when their daughter, Emmy, was only six months old. His parents had tried to get custody of the baby. When that didn't work they'd tried to kidnap her, which led to an assault charge being filed—against Georgia—for threatening her former mother-in-law with a chef's knife.

Georgia had spent three years on the run with Emmy, always looking over her shoulder. Marcus had put her together with a good lawyer, who had gotten a permanent restraining order against the Wylers, and slowly Georgia had begun to relax, at least a little.

"Maybe a cup of tea would be good," I said to Peggy.

"I'm going to get back to my lunch," Larry said, gesturing over his shoulder in the general direction of his table. He smiled at Georgia. "Would you let me walk you to your car when you leave? Please? For my own peace of mind?"

She nodded. "Yes. Thank you."

Larry went back to his table. I thought about how much he was like his father.

"I'm overreacting," Georgia said, sitting down on one of the vinyl-covered stools at the counter and pulling off her mittens. "Those kinds of encounters make me anxious."

"You're not overreacting and I think you handled things very well," I said, slipping onto the stool next to her. "I don't think I would have thought of stepping on his foot like that."

That got me a much bigger smile. "I saw that on *The Bachelorette*. Bianca stomped on Jarrod's foot when he stuck his tongue in her mouth." Color warmed the tops of her cheeks. "I watch it sometimes when I'm in the kitchen getting boxes ready for the cupcakes."

I leaned toward her. "Hercules and I watch the show while we fold laundry. Well, I do the folding. It's kind of tricky with paws." That made her smile.

Peggy came back with a cup of tea for Georgia and one for me as well. She gestured at the box of cupcakes. "You didn't have to bring these over today."

"No, it's okay," Georgia said. "I wanted you to have enough while I'm gone." She looked at me. "I'm going to Minneapolis for a few days to take a course. I'll be leaving tomorrow morning. I'm hoping to move into making cakes for special occasions, so I need to up my decorating skills." She turned her head toward the parking lot. "Maybe when I get back Mr. Wallace will be gone."

Peggy glanced over at the door again. "Lewis Wallace is a crass pig of a man. I don't think the town should be doing business with him and I intend to say so at the next town meeting." She straightened her rhinestone-tipped cat's-eye glasses. "The sooner that man is gone, the better."

I added a silent "amen" to that.

chapter 3

Hercules was sitting on the front steps when I got home. He watched as I got out of the truck and locked the driver's-side door.

"Let's go," I said, inclining my head in the direction of the backyard.

His response was to hold up one foot and shake it. I knew that was cat for "Carry me."

Hercules despised getting his feet wet. In fact, his dislike of having wet paws had led to him briefly being the not-so-proud owner of a pair of boots courtesy of Maggie. To be specific, black-and-white boots that matched his black-and-white fur, in a paw-print design complete with a soft fleece lining and an anti-slip sole. Maggie's heart had been in the right place but boots just weren't the right fashion choice for Hercules and he'd happily surrendered them to a cat in need at Roma's veterinarian clinic.

Harrison Taylor's other son, Harry, aka Young Harry or Harry Junior, had cleared the driveway and the walkway to the back door after the last storm. There were a few patches of half-melted snow on the path. There were also dry, bare spots, too. Hercules gave a pathetic meow, his left front paw still hanging in the air.

I blew out a breath, shifted my messenger bag to my left shoulder and scooped up the cat. "You are so spoiled," I told him. "Your character has been weakened."

"Mrrr," he said as he licked my chin. He didn't seem the slightest bit troubled by the idea.

We headed around the house to the back door. I set Hercules down on the steps, which were bare and dry, so I could fish my keys out of my pocket. He looked across the backyard toward Rebecca's house, narrowed his green eyes and began to make muttering noises. I knew what that was about.

"Everett will be back in a couple of days," I said as I opened the door. "You can go back to mooching bacon then."

My little house actually belonged to Everett Henderson. Living in it was a perk of taking the library job.

Back when I had first moved in, Everett and Rebecca weren't married. They weren't even seeing each other. They'd spent most of their lives loving each other but apart. The cats and I had played a very, very small role in getting them back together and for Everett that was a debt that could never be completely repaid.

After they were married Everett had moved into Rebecca's house and sold Wisteria Hill, his family home, to Roma. His "friendship" with Hercules had started with the two of them reading the newspaper over coffee (and bacon) in the backyard gazebo through the spring and summer. It was helped by the fact that Hercules looked just like Everett's late mother's cat, Finn. And it seemed Hercules—like Everett—had some strong opinions on town government.

Things had progressed to breakfast in the house on Tuesdays and Fridays during the colder months when Everett was in town—which he hadn't been for the past several days. I had no idea how the cat knew what day of the week it was, but he definitely did. For all I knew Hercules was looking at the calendar. Given everything else he was capable of, it wasn't exactly impossible.

I followed him into the kitchen, happy that he'd stopped and waited for me to open the door. He stretched and headed for his water dish. There was no sign of Owen. Or of Ethan, for that matter. They were both equally capable of getting into trouble and I had about as much control over the cat as I did over my baby brother.

"I'm home," I called. Usually that got me an answering meow at least, but there was nothing but silence. Had Owen gone out when Ethan left to meet me for lunch?

I kicked off my boots and was hanging up my jacket when I saw movement out of the corner of my eye. The basement door, which had been open just a crack, swung open a little wider and Owen poked his head into the room. There were bits of catnip on his whiskers and a piece of yellow fluff dangling from one ear. And his eyes didn't quite focus. I knew if I went down to the basement I'd find the remains of a Fred the Funky Chicken, yet another in a long line of yellow catnip chickens that Owen had decapitated.

Hercules looked at his brother, exhaled through his nose in a way that sounded like a small exclamation of disgust and exited through the kitchen door—literally this time—into the porch.

I crouched down next to Owen and brushed the flakes of catnip off of his whiskers and fur. "You have a monkey—no, scratch that—a chicken on your back," I said to him as I collared the bit of yellow fluff. He put one paw on my knee, gave my chin an awkward butt with his head and then very noisily got a drink before weaving his way out of the room.

I changed my clothes, threw a load of laundry in the washer and cleaned up the catnip and bits of funky chicken from the stairs and basement floor because who was I kidding, there was no way Owen was going to do it. Then I went back upstairs, rooted around to see what was in the fridge and the cupboards and decided to make apple spice muffins. Once the muffins were in the oven, I pulled out the vacuum.

Finally, I sat down at the table with my laptop and a cup of hot chocolate. Hercules had retreated upstairs when I'd gone out into the porch with the vacuum cleaner. Now he poked his head around the living room door and meowed inquiringly at me.

"All done," I said.

He padded over to the table and launched himself onto my lap.

"Remember the drunken man from last night that I told you about?" I asked. I talked to the cats a lot. Saying what I was thinking out loud helped me sort things out in my own mind; at least that's what I told myself.

Hercules gave a murp of acknowledgment.

"His name is Lewis Wallace. I want to see what I can find out about him." I raised an eyebrow at him. "Want to help me?"

"Merow!" he said. Hercules was almost always enthusiastic about helping me look things up online. He'd squint at the screen as though he were reading an article or examining a photograph. More than one stray swipe of his paw at the keyboard had somehow taken me to exactly the piece of information I needed.

It turned out there was a lot of information to be found online about the former football star. Wallace had played in the Canadian Football League for six years with three different teams. The offensive lineman's behavior had been offensive off the field, as well, at times. There had been multiple complaints from the cheerleaders for two of those teams about Wallace making inappropriate comments and getting handsie with them. He had also been fined several times for breaking curfew and for showing up late on two occasions for training camp when he was with the Montreal Alouettes, both of which he blamed on his chronic insomnia, which often left him wandering around in the middle of the night at whatever hotel the team was staying.

Given Wallace's checkered past and how easy it had been to find that information, I was surprised that the development committee was considering going into business with the man. Maybe this at least partly explained why coming to a final decision was taking so long.

It turned out that the supplement business wasn't the only deal Lewis Wallace had in the works. He and two partners were also in negotiations to lease a failed marina they co-owned on the Ohio River to a group that wanted to base a riverboat casino out of the space. Wallace had owned the property since his playing days in Canada.

Hercules sat on my lap and seemed to read each new screen that came up. When I reached for my cup he put a paw to the keyboard, then turned and looked expectantly at me. We seemed to have landed on a fan forum. I read a few posts and very quickly realized that Lewis Wallace had been a very polarizing player as far as the Canadian fans were concerned. Some had praised his play and excused his off-the-field exploits as nothing more than a young man letting off a little steam. The expression "boys will be boys" was used more than once.

Others had been critical because Wallace wasn't always willing to sign autographs, and several posters felt he was just lazy. Wallace had never seemed to work out in the off-season and his diet had been crappy because of his rabid sweet tooth.

I stretched and got up to switch the laundry from the washer to the dryer. When I came back upstairs Hercules was standing on his back legs, one white-tipped paw resting on the edge of the table while he studied the computer screen. I picked him up again, sat down and waited while he got settled.

There was an article from an Ottawa newspaper's website on the screen. It appeared to be about Lewis Wallace's life since retirement.

"How did you get here?" I asked the cat. He looked pointedly at the touch pad and then at me. Being a cat, he didn't say, "Well, duh," but it was implied.

After he retired Wallace had been involved in an online memorabilia business that went under, leaving disgruntled customers behind. There were accusations from clients that not all the items that had been on the company website were legit—several pieces turned out to be fakes and some others had been obtained through some sketchy means.

"Lewis Wallace doesn't sound like someone who's very responsible," I said.

"Mrr," Hercules agreed without moving his gaze from the laptop.

There was a link to another newspaper article at the end of

the one about Wallace's business dealings. I clicked on it. From a quick skim of the second piece I learned that the former football player had lost both of his parents within six months of each other when he was just nineteen.

I shifted Herc on my lap, leaning back so I could stroke the soft black fur on the top of his head. I thought about myself at nineteen. I had been so eager to get away from home and so lost and homesick once I actually had.

"That might explain why he acts a lot like a bratty teenager," I said. I wasn't condoning kicking a dog or harassing women but I wondered what kind of person I would have turned out to be without my mom and dad.

Hercules cocked his head to one side and wrinkled his nose. He didn't seem quite as convinced.

I shut down the computer and set Hercules on the floor. The dryer was about to buzz. At the meeting I'd gone to we'd learned that Lewis Wallace had bought a small organic supplement business. He was looking to expand, to set up a home base for the company as well as a distribution center. Mayville Heights was one of the possible sites.

"I remember Thorsten saying that we had a bit of an advantage because many of Wallace's suppliers are in this area, but that Wallace was looking for some pretty significant tax breaks from the town," I said to Hercules as he followed me down to the dryer. "The thing that sticks in my mind was that the presentation was a little short on hard numbers and firm timelines. And I don't remember anyone mentioning that failed memorabilia business." Had Lewis Wallace's obnoxious behavior contributed to its failure? I wondered.

❧

Ethan was back in time for supper. Milo and Derek were with him. I fed them chicken tortilla soup. Ethan made corn bread and the guys did the dishes.

"When are you going to join the twenty-first century and get a dishwasher?" Ethan teased as he put the bowls away in the cupboard.

"As long as you're here I have one," I countered.

We hadn't had a dishwasher when Ethan and Sara were little and they had taken turns drying and putting things away while I washed each night. Cleaning glasses, plates, bowls, cutlery *and* pots and pans for five people should have turned me off of doing dishes for life, but I'd had some of my best conversations with my brother and sister during those times. For me there was nothing tedious about washing dishes by hand, just lots of great memories. If nothing else, it was a good time for thinking while my hands were busy.

"Hey, Kathleen, how did the furry dudes get their names?" Milo asked, dipping his head in the cats' direction. He was the one up to his elbows in soapsuds.

Ethan turned to look at me. "Yeah, good question. How did you pick their names?"

Both cats turned to look at us as though they knew they were the topic of conversation.

"I was reading *A Prayer for Owen Meany*," I said, "and every time I went to pick up the book Owen was sitting on it. So I named him Owen."

"What about Hercules?" Milo said.

"He was named after the Roman god, the son of Zeus."

"So they got book names," Ethan said.

I nodded. That was true, for the most part. I didn't add that Hercules was actually named for the particular incarnation of the Roman god on the cheesy nineties' TV show *Hercules: The Legendary Journeys*. I knew I'd never hear the end of it if Ethan had that piece of information.

Once the kitchen had been cleaned, Ethan and Milo decided to drive over to Red Wing to check out a club. "My turn to be the dee-dee," Milo said.

"What's a dee-dee?" I asked.

"Designated driver," Ethan said over his shoulder. He turned and grinned at me. "Don't worry, big sister. We won't do anything irresponsible."

"I'm glad to hear that," I said, getting to my feet. I leaned in close to Milo. "I have bail money if you need it," I stage-whispered.

They all laughed, all except Derek, who was sitting at the table seemingly lost in thought, humming quietly to himself.

"Dude, are you coming with us?" Ethan asked.

Derek didn't respond. I wasn't sure if he hadn't heard Ethan or didn't realize the question had been directed at him.

Ethan leaned over and waved a hand in front of his friend's

face. Derek started and looked at Ethan, giving his head a shake. "Umm, scrambled," he said.

I could tell by the confused look in his eyes that he had no idea what he'd just been asked.

"I wasn't asking about breakfast," Ethan said. He and Milo were struggling not to laugh. And failing for the most part.

I caught Milo's eye. "Forty-two," I said.

He thought for a moment and then comprehension flashed across his face. He smiled, nodding. "Well, of course," he said, holding out both hands.

Now it was Ethan's turn to look confused. "Hey, some of us have no idea what you're talking about," he said.

"The Hitchhiker's Guide to the Galaxy," Milo said.

Ethan shrugged. "Sorry, I don't get it."

"Me neither," Derek said.

"In the book, 'forty-two' is the answer to the ultimate question about life, the universe, everything," I said.

"The only problem is no one knows what the question is," Milo finished.

Ethan still looked lost. I got up, put my arms around his shoulders and gave him a sideways hug. "Read the book," I said.

He stuck his tongue out at me, but I knew he would find the book.

"So you coming or what?" Ethan said to Derek.

Derek swiped a hand over his stubbled chin. "I don't think so," he said. "I really need to do a little more work on this song."

Ethan and Milo exchanged a look. "Better find Derek's

fanny pack," Milo said. He was leaning against the counter, surreptitiously—he seemed to think—dropping sardine crackers down to Owen and Hercules, who also seemed to think I didn't know what was going on. Milo had also absentmindedly eaten two of the crackers himself. I was waiting to share *that* particular piece of information with him.

Milo looked at me. "Hey, Kathleen, if later on tonight you see Derek wandering along the street, make sure you steer him back to the place we're staying or he could end up in, oh, I don't know"—he looked around the kitchen as though he was trying to orient himself—"say, Michigan."

"Driving here we almost did end up in Michigan," Derek retorted. "Thanks to you and your cheapo GPS." He smirked. "Turn left in two, two, two, two, two miles," he mimicked a stilted robotic voice.

"There's nothing wrong with your writing style, Derek," I said, folding my hands on Ethan's shoulder and resting my head on them. "It's better than someone's technique, which is to sit around unshaven in his tighty-whities, eating Cheetos and burping."

Ethan twisted out of my grasp. "I do not sit around in my underwear burping when I'm writing a song," he said, his voice indignant.

I held up my phone. "I beg to differ and I have the video to prove it."

"There's no way you have that video because Sara would never have given it to you."

I gave an elaborately casual shrug. "I don't mind showing you."

Ethan's mouth moved like he was tasting his words before he spoke them. "Fine," he said. He held up a finger. "Once, once I might have been working on a song first thing in the morning before I had a chance to put on a pair of pants. One time, and certain people"—he glared at me—"never let you forget it."

Milo made a face. "Man, I don't care what your process is, but I could have gone for the rest of my life not knowing that you wear tighty-whities."

The guys laughed and Ethan slung an arm around my shoulders. "You better sleep with one eye open, big sister, because I am going to get you for this." He was grinning, too, so I knew he wasn't angry with me. I also knew that didn't mean he wouldn't try to get even. On the other hand, if anyone else even hinted at coming after me for any reason, real or imagined, my little brother was my fiercest defender.

For a moment my chest tightened, as though I'd pulled on a too-tight sweater. I'd missed this, Ethan and his friends, cooking, eating and teasing one another. Ethan razzing me about Bigfoot sightings on the phone wasn't the same thing.

As if he could read my mind, he leaned over and dropped a kiss on the top of my head. "I'm glad I'm here," he said in a quiet voice.

I nodded. "Me too."

Milo had run out of crackers, so both Owen and Hercules

had disappeared. I was guessing Hercules had gone upstairs to prowl around in my closet while Owen was likely in the basement rooting in his catnip chicken stash.

"So what's your plan for the morning?" I asked Ethan. He and Derek were teaching a one-day songwriting workshop at the St. James Hotel on Sunday.

"Can I get a ride down with you? Milo wants the van. He's going to some flea market place Maggie told him about." He smiled.

"Sure," I said. "My meeting's at nine."

"Why so early and why on a Sunday?" He held up a hand. "Not that it's too early for me. Derek and I need to get stuff set up."

"There's a quilt festival coming up. It's mostly centered at the library but there will be a big product show and tea at the hotel. Things need to be moved back and forth. I have to go over the schedule and coordinate with Melanie, the hotel manager, and tomorrow morning is the only time we could make work for both of our schedules."

"Yeah, Derek talked to her when he was getting this workshop set up. The whole thing was pretty much his idea."

I glanced over at Derek, who was showing Milo something on his phone. "Well, since it's keeping you around longer, I'm glad," I said.

"You know, when Jake said he was going back to school I was afraid we were going to be screwed," Ethan said, sliding the leather cord bracelet he wore up his arm. "But he was actually the one who suggested we at least hear Derek play. One time was all it took. Lucky for us he was looking to make some extra money. You heard him say his kid is headed to college in the fall."

I nodded.

"Don't get me wrong, Derek can rub people the wrong way sometimes and, yeah, there are lots of days I wish Jake was still with us, but I've learned a ton in the past couple of months. My guitar playing is better. So's my songwriting."

"I'm glad it worked out," I said, "and I'm sure the two of you will be a big hit tomorrow."

Ethan grinned. "You might be a little biased, but thanks for the vote of confidence."

Marcus arrived just as the guys were leaving.

"Do I have time for a shower?" I heard Milo say.

"You don't need to wash your hair," Ethan replied. "It looks fine and it smells like a piña colada. You're good."

I didn't hear Milo's response.

Marcus set a small brown paper shopping bag on the table. Both cats appeared in the kitchen, sitting side by side next to the table, green eyes and golden eyes fixed on the paper bag. "What makes you think there's something in that bag for you?" I asked.

Owen shot me a look.

"I had this coupon for fifty cents off a can of sardines," Marcus began, fishing in the bag.

"And you didn't want it to go to waste," I finished.

"Something like that." He at least had the good grace to look a bit embarrassed.

We'd been a couple for a year and a half now but I was still learning things about him. For instance, I'd recently discovered he liked samurai movies. Tonight we were going to watch one of his favorites: *13 Assassins*. It seemed fair. He'd sat through one of my favorite movies, *Santa Claus Conquers the Martians,* at Christmastime. Marcus had promised popcorn with the movie. I knew that was a bribe.

I sat at the table while Marcus made the popcorn at the stove. After they had made quick work of their respective sardine halves the boys joined me, Hercules on my lap because he'd be closer to the popcorn when Marcus eventually set it on the table and Owen at my feet, which was his preferred spot in case any buttery kernels landed on the floor, which had been known to happen. Sometimes actually by accident.

Marcus was on a popcorn kick and had been since Christmas, when his sister, Hannah, had sent him some organic popcorn from a little company in Illinois. Now instead of making popcorn in the microwave he made it on the stove, dousing it with melted butter and sea salt, both of which he bought at the weekend farmer's market.

"Hannah had no idea she was creating a popcorn snob when she sent you that original bag," I said as the aroma of melting butter filled the kitchen. Hercules's whiskers twitched as I stroked his fur.

Marcus put one hand on his chest in faux indignation. "I'm

not a snob, I'm an aficionado," he said. Right on cue Owen meowed his agreement.

"You have an opinion on everything, don't you?" I said to the cat.

He licked his whiskers. He definitely had an opinion on anything with melted butter.

I leaned back in the chair, one hand on Hercules, who sighed softly. He knew there was pretty much no chance either of them was getting any popcorn; still, he liked licking butter and salt off my fingers, so for him this whole process was taking way too long.

"Did you know that the US is the world's largest producer of popcorn?" I asked.

"No, I did not." Marcus tipped his head toward the covered pot he was shaking over the burner. I wasn't sure what he was listening for. Then again, I was happy with a bag of popcorn made in the microwave.

"It comes in two shapes, you know," I continued. "Snow-flake and mushroom. Because snowflake-shaped popcorn is bigger, movie theaters typically sell that shape."

He was smiling at me, I realized.

"Am I talking too much?"

He stretched sideways to kiss the top of my head. "No, you're not," he said. He straightened up and turned his attention back to the stove. "Remember Lewis Wallace, the drunk from last night? Turns out he's had some dealings with the police."

"The memorabilia business," I said. "How did you find out?"

"Guy from the prosecutor's office was at the bar. He recognized Wallace. How did you find out?"

I gave him a brief rundown of my two encounters with Lewis Wallace and my subsequent research online. "I don't know if any of this is relevant to Wallace bringing his business to town," I said. "It's not as though the information was hard to find. And let's be realistic. The town can't make some kind of character test a requirement for anyone who might set up business here."

Hercules nudged my hand because I had stopped scratching between his ears.

"Still, I was thinking maybe I should talk to Lita. Or do you think the whole story about what happened last night is pretty much around town by now?"

Marcus frowned at the popcorn, which was now in a large bowl. He added a sprinkle more salt. "I'd be surprised if the story *weren't* all around town by this point," he said. He gave the bowl a shake and nodded, seemingly satisfied. "You're right that we can't set some kind of moral code that people have to meet just to be in business, because I'm pretty sure that would be a small pool, but on the other hand it doesn't benefit the town to make a deal with someone that no one else will want to work with." He gave me a wry smile. "Roma is on that development committee, remember? I'm going out to Wisteria Hill tomorrow to help Eddie get some stuff down out of the attic. I'll tell her what happened—last night and today—and see what she thinks."

Roma and I had met when Hercules and Owen followed me home from Wisteria Hill, two little balls of fur that didn't seem to have a mother. That was back when Everett Henderson still owned the place. Later, Roma recruited me to join her team of volunteers that helped take care of the feral cat colony that lived in the old carriage house on the property. "Coincidentally" she'd paired me with Marcus.

Roma had married former NHL star Eddie Sweeney this past summer. They were still in the happily-ever-after honeymoon phase and I'd been surprised when she'd agreed to get involved with the new business committee the town had put together. But since I knew she'd be the calm voice of reason I was selfishly happy she'd said yes.

I got to my feet, gave Marcus a kiss and swiped a handful of popcorn from the bowl. "That works for me," I said.

I was awakened in the morning by a poke from a furry paw. I opened one eye to find a furry black-and-white face looming over mine. I groaned. Hercules looked from me to my old clock radio and back again. I threw an arm over my eyes. "Yes, I know I wanted to get up early but not this early," I told him. Despite the fact that the time change meant it was six thirty, to me it still felt like half past five.

I lay there for a moment and I could feel the cat still lurking. "You win," I said, sitting up. Hercules dropped to all four feet and headed to the door. He paused in the doorway and gave a loud murp. Hercules liked to get the last word.

I got dressed and went down to the kitchen to make the coffee and feed Owen and Hercules their breakfast. I was leaning against the counter, both hands wrapped around my coffee mug, when Ethan wandered in, bare-chested, wearing just a pair of blue plaid-flannel pajama pants, his dark hair standing on end just the way it had when he was a little boy.

"How about a T-shirt?" I said, grabbing a mug from the counter and offering it to him. "No one wants to see that first thing in the morning."

He reached for the coffeepot, poured a cup and then grinned at me. He rubbed a hand over his belly. "I haven't had any complaints so far."

I made a face at him. "Way, way more information than I need to have."

Ethan just continued to smirk as he added cream and sugar to his mug.

I scrambled three eggs with some spinach and we ate them with the muffins I'd made the day before. Ethan told me about the band they'd gone to hear and I told him about the samurai movie. It seemed the movie had been a lot better than the music.

We headed down to the hotel about quarter to nine.

"So this is *Old* Main Street?" Ethan said when we turned the corner at the bottom of the hill.

I nodded. "Which is not the same as *Main* Street."

"How the heck did that happen?"

"Would you believe I'm not sure?" I said. I'd gotten confused more than once, trying to find my way around town when I'd first moved to Mayville Heights from Boston, mostly due to the way some of the streets and buildings were named—and sometimes renamed. For instance, Old Main Street followed the shoreline from the Stratton Theatre, past the library and the St. James Hotel all the way to the marina. *Main* Street continued from the marina to the edge of town, where it joined the highway. Having two Main Streets made giving directions to visitors a little complicated, compounded by the fact that the St. James Hotel had reverted to its original name after a decade of being just the James Hotel.

It struck me that maybe the question about the streets was something Harrison could answer in his next talk.

"How far does that walking trail go?" Ethan asked, gesturing at the Riverwalk.

For me, one of the best parts of the downtown was the Riverwalk, which ran along the waterfront with all the tall black walnut and elm trees that lined the shore. "The trail begins up by the old warehouses at the point," I said. "Then runs past the downtown shops and businesses, all the way out beyond the marina."

If Lewis Wallace made a deal with the city, one of those warehouses would be home to his company.

Derek was waiting out front of the St. James with his guitar.

He looked tired, with sooty dark circles under his eyes and lines pulling at the corners of them. There was a tiny bit of stubble on his chin that he'd missed shaving.

"How's the song coming?" I asked.

"Umm, slowly," he said.

"You want me to take a look at what you have so far?" Ethan asked.

Derek shook his head. "Give me a little more time to chew on it."

Ethan shrugged. "No problem."

Melanie Davis was waiting for us at the front desk. Melanie and I had originally met when I'd had to collect an intoxicated Burtis Chapman—Brady's dad—and Marcus's father, Elliot Gordon, from the hotel bar, where, lubricated with a fair amount of alcohol, they had been entertaining the customers with their vocal skills. When she joined the library board I was glad to get to know her in less embarrassing circumstances.

"Melanie, this is my brother, Ethan," I said, "and you already know Derek Hanson."

She smiled. "Ethan, it's good to meet you, and Derek, it's good to meet you in person." Melanie was about my height, curvy with smooth brown skin, dark eyes and gorgeous corkscrew curls to her shoulders.

"It's good to meet you, too," Ethan said.

Derek simply nodded.

Melanie turned to me. "Kathleen, do you mind me showing

Derek and Ethan their meeting room first and then we can go to my office?"

"That's fine with me," I said.

She led us across the lobby and down a hallway to the left. Derek had his guitar. Ethan carried his own guitar and a messenger bag I knew was full of papers. We stopped at a door at the end of the hall. I knew the room had big windows that overlooked the garden in the back of the hotel and would fill the space with light. It would be a great place for the workshop.

Melanie pulled out a set of keys. "These are the original doors." She raised an eyebrow. "They add 'character,' so there's a key as well as a code. Once we check the setup of the room I'll input a temporary code the two of you can use for the day to secure the room at lunchtime if you want to leave for a while."

"Thank you," Ethan said.

"I should warn you that there are no security cameras in this part of the hotel. They're coming once the renovation work makes it to this floor."

"You're upgrading the entire building," I said.

She nodded. "Right now, they're working on the floor above us. I actually have a temporary office on this main floor." She pointed north down another corridor. "My office and several others are getting a face-lift. All the executive offices will be together and we're getting two renovated washrooms. And eventually all of these old doors will be replaced with a keycard system."

"You'll lose a little character," I said.

"The downside of updates," she said. She gestured at the meeting room door. "The tables and chairs are set up the way we talked about and there's a big whiteboard," Melanie continued. "We can also get you a couple of smaller portable ones if you think you'll need them."

"Umm, no, one should be fine," Ethan said.

"One of the kitchen staff will bring hot water and coffee about fifteen minutes before you start," Melanie continued as she put the key in the lock. "They'll bring more hot water and fresh coffee before you begin your afternoon session." She glanced over her shoulder at us. "In my experience people like to get a cup of coffee or tea before they get started." She swung the paneled door open and then froze in the open doorway, her breath catching in her throat. I took a couple of steps closer to see what was wrong with the meeting room.

The problem wasn't the room. The problem was Lewis Wallace slumped at one of the tables. Even from where I was standing it was pretty clear he was dead.

chapter 4

The color had drained from Melanie's face. "We have to do something," she said, taking a step forward. I caught her arm and she turned to look at me, clearly confused. "Kathleen, that's . . . that's . . ." She stopped and swallowed hard. "I know him. His name . . ." She cleared her throat. "His name is Lewis Wallace."

"He's past our help," I said quietly. "I'm sorry."

"What's going on?" Ethan asked, a frown creasing his forehead. He leaned sideways a bit and because he was taller he could see Wallace's body. He swore softly under his breath. "Kathleen, is that . . . ?"

I nodded. "Call nine-one-one," I said. "Please."

"Are you positive he's . . . dead?" Ethan asked. "Someone should make sure."

"I'll uh . . . I'll check." The way Wallace's body was slumped over at the table, the mottled color of the skin on the side of his face that was visible told me he'd been dead for a while, but I made my way over to him and felt for a pulse at his neck. As I'd expected, I didn't find one. This wasn't my first dead body.

I glanced back over my shoulder at Ethan and shook my head.

He nodded, took a few steps away from us and pulled out his phone.

I took a quick look around the meeting room. There was a box from Sweet Things on the table. A chair was overturned and I saw pieces of a broken glass on the floor next to Wallace's feet. Had Wallace done that or had there been some sort of struggle with someone else?

Across the room I spotted what looked like an orange-capped pen against the leg of the whiteboard stand. Nothing else seemed to be out of place. I stepped back and pulled the door shut.

Melanie seemed to have regained her composure. She swallowed a couple of times and stood up a little straighter. "I'm sorry, Kathleen," she said. She cleared her throat and stared at the closed door. "I've just never seen a dead body before."

I gave her arm a squeeze. "It's okay," I said. She'd said she knew Lewis Wallace. I wondered what their connection was.

As if she'd read my thoughts, she turned her gaze back to

me. "I . . . worked with Lew, briefly, years ago. Before he showed up here at the hotel a few days ago I hadn't seen him in years."

Ethan walked back over to us. "The police are on their way."

"Someone should meet them at the front entrance," Melanie said. "This is going to be upsetting for some of the guests. I, uh . . . I'm not exactly sure what I'm going to tell them."

"If anyone asks all you have to say is that a guest was taken ill," I said. "It's true as far as any of us know at the moment."

Melanie nodded. "That's a good idea. Thank you." She looked at the door. "I should probably lock that just to be safe."

"Good idea," I said.

Melanie relocked the door. She smoothed her black pencil skirt. "I'm going to wait out front," she said. "If any of the staff show up just send them out to find me."

Ethan couldn't seem to stop moving. He'd been pacing back and forth in the hallway, hands going to the cord bracelet around his wrist, to his phone, raking through his hair, picking at his shirt. He looked at me now. "That Wallace guy, he's *dead* dead? For real? Are you sure?"

I looked at him without speaking and he seemed to remember who he was talking to. "Never mind. I'm sorry. Forget it," he said, waving one hand in the air as though he were trying to wave the words away.

Derek was leaning against the wall, his guitar propped next to him. He was so pale I thought he might pass out. "I didn't want him to end up dead," he said.

SOFIE KELLY

I nodded. "I know. The man was a jerk but nobody wanted him to die."

I turned my attention back to Ethan. It seemed to me that I could feel the nervous energy he was giving off the same way that I could feel the heat from Harrison Taylor's woodstove when I sat beside it.

"Do you have a class list and contact information for your students?" I asked.

He stopped pacing to look at me. "Yes," he said and it seemed to dawn on him that people were due to be arriving soon. "What am I going to say to them?"

"Just say that due to unforeseen circumstances you have to cancel the workshop. Apologize for it being last minute and say that you'll be issuing refunds in the next twenty-four hours." I slipped my messenger bag onto my other shoulder. "You can do that, can't you?"

Ethan thought for a moment but Derek was already nodding. "We can do that."

"You probably should get started, then," I said.

The two of them bent their heads over Ethan's phone.

I rubbed my stomach with one hand. It ached. It was a familiar feeling.

The responding police officer was Officer Stephen Keller, ex-military, tall, square-shouldered and serious. We'd met under these types of circumstances before. He gave me a quick nod of recognition.

The paramedics were right behind him. I recognized them

as well, Ric Holm and his partner. Ric and I had first met when I'd been injured escaping from a house just seconds before it exploded. I awakened wrapped in blankets on a stretcher in the back of an ambulance with a very pissed-off Owen sitting on my stomach and Ric beside me. It was the first time he'd given me first aid but as it turned out it hadn't been the last.

Melanie had returned with Officer Keller and was unlocking the meeting room door.

"So what's going on?" Ric asked. He wore navy blue pants that must have had at least half a dozen pockets and a short-sleeved navy shirt with a patch on one shoulder that said *Mayville Heights Paramedic.* A stethoscope was draped around his neck.

"There's a man inside, dead at one of the tables. His name is Lewis Wallace," I said. I held on to the strap of my messenger bag, running my hand along the tightly woven webbing.

"Did you check for a pulse?" Ric asked.

I nodded. "I couldn't find one. And . . . and I know what someone looks like when they're dead."

Melanie opened the door and Ric and his partner quickly made their way over to Lewis Wallace followed by Officer Keller, who shut the door behind them. The two paramedics weren't in the room very long. Ric came out, pulling off a pair of blue latex gloves. "Is everyone okay out here?" he asked, looking around.

"We're good, Ric," I said. "Thanks."

"Take care, Kathleen," he said. "I hope next time I see you it's under better circumstances."

I nodded. "Me too."

Marcus arrived then. He put a hand on my shoulder. "You all right?" he asked, keeping his voice low.

"We're all fine," I said.

"What's going on?" He was already pulling a pair of gloves similar to Ric's from his pocket.

I explained briefly what had happened, how Ethan and Derek were supposed to be giving a workshop and I'd had a meeting planned with Melanie. She nodded in agreement.

"Melanie was just going to let Ethan and Derek into the room—this room—and then the two of us were going to her office to talk about the quilt show," I continued. "She opened the door and we both saw Wallace. I checked but he was already dead. I'm the only person who actually went into the room."

Marcus's blue eyes narrowed. "Wait a minute. Did you say Wallace? Do you mean Lewis Wallace?"

I nodded.

He pressed his lips together for a moment. "Everyone, please, just stay here," he said.

There was a long wooden bench in the main hallway in front of an emergency exit and a bank of floor-to-ceiling windows. I sat down. I knew we were going to be a while.

Things got busy after that. Marcus came back out after a few minutes, talking on his cell. He had more questions for both Melanie and me. He spoke briefly to Ethan and Derek. They hadn't seen much so that didn't take very long. By then the crime scene techs had arrived.

Marcus spoke to one of them and finally came back and stood in front of me. I got to my feet. "You can go home, Kathleen," he said. "I told your brother and Derek to stay around because I'll need to talk to all three of you later. You know how these things work."

I did know. I wished I didn't. "We'll stay at the house," I said. "Call me when you get a chance."

"I will," he said and his hand brushed mine for a second.

I promised Melanie that I'd call her and we'd reschedule. I collected Ethan and Derek and we headed home. No one said a word on the drive up the hill.

"Marcus is going to have more questions for us later," I warned as I pulled into the driveway. Derek was sitting close to the passenger door. I looked around Ethan. "Derek, why don't you stay here for a while?"

He swiped a hand over his face. "Yeah, I think I will. Thanks."

There was no sign of Owen or Hercules. I knew the latter could be anywhere given his ability to come and go as he pleased. Owen had to be somewhere in the house. I had my fingers crossed that he wouldn't "appear" at the wrong time.

We'd been home for about fifteen minutes and I'd just poured myself a cup of coffee when Maggie called.

"I heard what happened," she said. "I'm making pizza. Don't make any plans for lunch."

I leaned against the counter. "Thank you," I said. I hadn't even thought about lunch. "Oh, Ethan and Derek are here."

"It's okay. It's a big pizza," she said.

Ethan had come out to the kitchen while I was talking to Mags. He poured himself a cup of coffee. It struck me that our coffee habit was another way we both took after our mother. Thea Paulson was beautiful, charismatic, opinionated and stubborn. All three of us had inherited that stubborn streak. Ethan definitely had Mom's stage presence and charisma.

My parents had each been married twice. Both times to each other. Ethan and Sara were the result of their reconciliation. I was fifteen and mortified by the undeniable proof that my mother and father, who I'd thought were barely on speaking terms, were actually much closer than that.

"That was Maggie," I said, ending the phone call. "She's bringing pizza."

A smile flashed across Ethan's face. I didn't think it was because of the pizza. It wasn't my overprotective big-sister imagination. Ethan had a bit of a crush on Maggie. I opened my mouth to say something and took a sip of coffee instead. This wasn't the time.

"I'm going to make a couple of phone calls," Ethan said. His hair was sticking up all over his head. I caught myself reaching out to smooth it down the way I had done when he was a kid and stopped myself. Ethan wasn't a kid anymore and I needed to remember that.

I poked my head in the living room, where Derek was sitting on the sofa with his laptop. "Coffee's ready," I said.

He gave me a tight smile, or what passed for a smile at the

moment. "Thanks," he said, setting the computer on the sofa cushion beside him and getting to his feet. He looked tired and a bit gray. Unlike Ethan, who burned off his stress by constantly being in motion, it seemed that Derek kept what he was feeling inside. He poured a cup of coffee, added two sugars and stirred distractedly as he checked his phone. His mouth pulled to one side and he jammed the phone in the pocket of his jeans.

"Is everything all right?" I asked.

Derek let out a breath. "Yeah. Liam hasn't answered my text." He shook his head. "Kids."

"What does he want to study in college?" I said, mostly to fill the silence.

"Communications or maybe recreation. It doesn't matter." Derek made a dismissive gesture with one hand.

"It doesn't?" The confusion I was feeling had to be showing on my face.

"Liam's going to play in the NFL. What he studies doesn't make any difference." Derek took a sip of his coffee. "We're headed for the big time. All that other stuff is just background noise." He took his cup and went back to the living room.

A college education was just background noise? Once again I found myself missing Jake and his scraps of paper covered with pencil sketches.

I decided I'd go over the plans for the quilt show and see what information I could e-mail to Melanie. I sat down at the kitchen table and Owen suddenly appeared at my feet, a little too suddenly. He launched himself onto my lap, peered at my cup and then looked around. As far as Owen was concerned a cup of coffee was an excuse for a brownie or a cookie or even a piece of toast with peanut butter. He loved peanut butter.

"No treats," I said, stroking the top of his head.

He made a murp of dissatisfaction.

"Maggie's bringing pizza later."

Immediately, he lifted a paw and took a couple of passes at his face. "You look very handsome," I assured him.

Owen loved Maggie—something he and Ethan had in common it seemed. Owen followed her everywhere, sat with a rapt look of adoration at her feet and had on more than one occasion dispatched an errant rodent, which in turn meant that Maggie was also crazy about him. She—along with Rebecca— kept him in catnip chickens and sympathized with him over his antipathy toward the music of Mr. Barry Manilow, whom both Hercules and I adored. Aside from the fact that Owen and Maggie were different species, it was a perfect friendship.

Owen looked over the papers spread on the table in front of me. He switched his gaze to me and then cocked his head to one side and meowed, it seemed to me, in curiosity.

I felt self-conscious about having a conversation with a cat when Ethan and Derek were around although I did it all the time when I was by myself. "I'll tell you later, I promise," I whispered. That seemed to satisfy him.

Maggie arrived just before noon with the pizza.

"It smells wonderful," I said.

"It should go in the oven for about five minutes," she said, kicking off her boots and coming into the kitchen in the wildly striped socks that Ella King had knit for her.

"I thought you might say that, so I've already warmed it up."

With the pizza in the oven Maggie shrugged off her coat and scarf and leaned down to say hello to Owen.

"Hey, Maggie," Ethan said, coming in from the living room. He'd combed his hair and changed his shirt.

I wasn't sure how I felt about my baby brother having a crush on one of my best friends. Not good, that was for sure, which made me feel guilty. Where was the harm? Since I'd been a teenager when Ethan and Sara were born my role had been part older sister, part second mother. More than once Ethan had reminded me that he already had a mother and she was more than enough.

"Hi," Maggie said with a smile. Ethan took her coat and hung it up. Maggie snagged a little brown paper bag from one of the pockets. I knew what was inside.

"No, no, no," I said, shaking my head.

Ethan looked confused. "What?" he asked.

"You're spoiling him."

Now Ethan looked completely lost. "How is Maggie spoiling me? What did she do?"

"Not you," I said. "Owen."

The cat in question also knew what was in the bag. His golden eyes were locked on Maggie.

She took Fred the Funky Chicken out of the bag, leaned down and held it out. Owen took it carefully from her. The half-lidded look he gave her was pure bliss.

"Mrrr," he said as he headed for the living room.

"You're welcome," Maggie called after him with a smile. She cleared her throat and her smile faded. "I know it's Lewis Wallace who's dead," she said. "May he be welcomed by the light."

Once again news had traveled around town faster than a New York minute. Given the speed the information had spread, maybe the expression should have been "a Mayville Heights minute."

"I'm not going to ask what happened because I know Marcus probably told you not to talk about it," she said as she caught one of the chrome chairs with her foot and pulled it out so she could sit down.

"Thanks, Mags," I said, giving her a hug. "And for the record, when Owen decapitates that chicken—and he will—I'm calling you to clean it up!"

The pizza was fantastic as usual. Pizza making was one of Maggie's skills. She'd dirty every dish in her apartment but the end result was always worth the mess.

About halfway through the meal the conversation turned to the missed workshop.

"Any chance we'll be able to reschedule?" Maggie asked.

"Wait a minute," I said. "We? I didn't know you were taking the class."

She nodded, gesturing with her fork. "Ruby talked me into it."

Maggie was primarily a collage artist, although she also created detailed, fanciful drawings like the ones she'd done for the trail map of this area and the street map of the town. Ruby, on the other hand, created bold pop-art paintings in vivid neon colors and often hand-tinted her photographs.

"I didn't know you were interested in writing songs."

"I'm interested in the creative process in general," she said.

Ethan leaned forward, propping an elbow on the table. "What would you like to know?" he asked.

They started talking about songwriting and I just listened. Derek was quickly pulled into the conversation. Both Ethan's and Derek's mood lightened as they explained their writing process to Maggie. The dark cloud that had been hanging over us since we'd gotten home from the hotel seemed to dissipate as the three of them talked.

When Maggie finally had to leave for her shift at the co-op store I walked her out. "Thank you for the pizza and the conversation," I said.

"Anytime," she said with a smile. "I like your brother." Her expression changed. "I didn't like Lewis Wallace but I'm sorry he's dead." She gave me a hug, hopped into her Bug and drove away.

I thought about what Maggie had said and told myself that the niggling unsettling feeling I had was just that, an uncomfortable sensation that was understandable given that I had just seen a dead body a few hours ago.

❀

Marcus arrived midafternoon just as I was debating making cookies. He didn't kiss me, which I assumed was because Ethan was in the kitchen with me.

"Have you had lunch or would you at least like coffee?" I asked.

He gave me a tight smile. "I'm fine, thanks."

He seemed to be in working-cop mode, all business with very little of his emotions showing through.

"Is Derek here?" he asked.

"He went for a walk," I said. "He was getting a little antsy but he should be back anytime now," said. A knot was forming in my stomach. I tried to ignore it.

"I'll wait," Marcus said. "It'll give me time to go over both of your stories again."

I was just finishing explaining why I'd been so sure that Lewis Wallace was dead before I'd even checked for his pulse when Derek walked in. He seemed surprised to see Marcus.

"I need to ask you a few questions," Marcus said. "I'd like you to come down to the station with me, please."

"Why?" I said. The knot in my stomach was knitting itself into a giant lump. "Marcus, what's going on?"

"Is Derek under arrest?" Ethan asked. I didn't like the challenge in his voice or his expression.

"No one is under arrest," Marcus replied. "I just have some questions."

"Ask them here." Ethan's back was up. I could tell from his body language, legs wide apart, hands moving through the air.

"The station would be better." In contrast to Ethan, Marcus's voice was steady and quiet.

"It doesn't matter," Derek said. "I don't mind going." The pinched lines on his face told me that might not be the truth.

Ethan made a gesture with one hand like he was swatting a bug away. "No, it's not fine. They think you did this."

Marcus shook his head. "I didn't say that."

"You didn't have to," Ethan retorted. "It's pretty obvious."

I stepped between them. "It's because of what happened at the bar, isn't it?" I searched Marcus's blue eyes for some clue to what he was thinking.

"And the altercation in front of Eric's. Yes."

Derek's face reddened and he glanced down at his feet.

Marcus looked at Derek. "I just have to hear your side of things," he said. "On the record. That's all."

Derek looked up. "Really, it's fine," he repeated. He glanced at Ethan then shifted his attention to Marcus. "Let's just get this over with."

"Thank you," Marcus said.

Ethan pushed past me, blocking Derek's way. "Don't do this," he said between clenched teeth.

Derek shook his head. "It's okay. It's not like I wanted the guy dead." He reached for his jacket, which was hanging on the back of a chair.

I looked at Marcus. "Brady," he mouthed.

I gave an almost imperceptible nod and the two men left.

Ethan swore, turned away from the door and folded both arms up over his head. "Derek didn't do this," he said. "He wouldn't hurt anyone, even an asshole like that Wallace guy." He looked at me. "Go after Marcus. Talk to him. Do something!"

I reached for my phone, punched in a number and waited. "I am doing something," I said.

When Maggie answered I asked if Brady was with her, mentally crossing my fingers that he was.

"He's right here," she said. "Would you like to talk to him?"

"Please," I said.

Maggie handed over the phone to Brady and I gave him the highlights of what had just happened. "I know I'm interrupting your Sunday, and I'm putting you on the spot."

Brady laughed. "I wouldn't have gone to law school if I didn't want to be put on the spot. And you've met my father. Shy and quiet is not in our DNA. I'm on my way."

I thanked him and ended the call.

Ethan had been watching me. "That was Maggie's boyfriend or whatever the heck he is; Brady, right?"

"Yes, that was Brady; yes, he and Maggie are friends," I snapped. *And yes, you should stop mooning over her like some smitten teenage boy,* I added silently. "He's on his way to the station."

"You don't have to bite my head off."

"And you don't have to act like a child when Marcus is just doing his job," I said. I admired Ethan's loyalty to his friend but I also had the urge to shake him at the moment. His behavior hadn't helped anyone.

He pulled out his phone. "I need to let Milo know what's going on." There was a petulant set to his jaw.

I nodded, set my own phone on the table and decided I needed a bit of fresh air. "I'm just going outside for a minute."

Ethan's focus was on his phone. He lifted one hand to let me know he'd heard me but he didn't say anything.

"Ethan," I said.

He looked up at me then.

"For the record, Marcus is one of the good guys." I didn't wait for a response.

Hercules was sitting in his usual place by the window in the porch. I sat down next to him and explained what was going on. He made sympathetic noises. "You know what this means, don't you?" I said. "Whatever happened to Lewis Wallace wasn't an accident."

A bit more than an hour later Brady brought Derek back. Milo had arrived by then. Everyone had questions and they were all asking them at once. Brady stood in the middle of the kitchen and gave a piercing two-fingered whistle. The room went silent.

"All Marcus wanted was to ask some questions about the times Derek had encountered Lewis Wallace," Brady said. "He hasn't been charged with anything. He's not in any trouble."

"So does this mean that Wallace guy was murdered?" Milo asked.

"For now, all the police are saying is that he died under suspicious circumstances. They won't know anything for certain until the medical examiner does the autopsy."

"This could all turn out to be nothing, then," Ethan said.

"Yes," Derek said. "It's not a big deal. A man died. The police aren't sure what happened yet. They're just trying to piece together his last couple of days. That's it." He turned to Brady and offered his hand. "Thank you."

"No problem," Brady said.

They shook hands and I walked Brady out.

"Are things really okay?" I asked as we stood next to his truck in the driveway.

He nodded. "For the moment. Marcus did ask Derek to stay in town for now."

I felt a little frisson of anxiety and I rubbed the back of my neck. "He doesn't have an alibi, does he?"

The lines around Brady's mouth tightened. "What are you getting at?"

I folded my arms over my midsection. I was suddenly cold. "I checked Lewis Wallace to see if he was still alive. His body was stiff but still warm. That means he'd been dead for more than a couple of hours—probably closer to seven or eight." I hated that I knew that.

Brady sighed. "Derek says he couldn't sleep so he went out for a walk."

"Yeah, Ethan says Derek does that when he's working on a song and he gets stuck."

"In a bigger place someone probably would have seen him, but here . . ." He held up a hand and let it drop.

"Brady, did Marcus say anything about how Lewis Wallace died?" I thought about the quick glimpse of the meeting room I'd had. There was something I'd noticed: what I'd thought was an orange-capped pen on the floor on the far side of the room. Now I realized that it was more likely an EpiPen.

Brady shook his head. "He didn't. I really don't think he knows yet and if he has any suspicions he's keeping his cards close to his vest, as my dad would say." He smiled then. "Speaking of Dad, when are you coming out to the house to wax him again at pinball?"

I smiled. "Is he still making noise about a rematch?"

Brady's smile stretched from ear to ear. "Oh yeah." He was a pretty good player himself but not quite as good as I was. I'd spent a lot of time unsupervised as a kid.

"He still claiming the floor was uneven?"

"That, too."

Brady had bought a pinball machine at the weekend market several months ago. It was out at his father's house. Both Marcus and Burtis Chapman had bragged about their prowess on the machine. I'd told them I was pretty good as well. They hadn't taken me at my word. "Once this case is wrapped up I'll be out," I said.

"I'm holding you to that," Brady said, pointing a finger at me.

"Thanks for bailing me out, again, figuratively speaking," I said.

"Anytime," he said.

I went back inside and found Ethan waiting for me in the porch; Hercules was sitting beside him on the bench. They both looked up at me.

Ethan got right to the point. "Derek couldn't kill anybody."

Hercules meowed his agreement.

I rubbed my neck again. The knot in my shoulders was working its way up the back of my head. "No one said he did. Marcus is just doing his job. He's asking questions and gathering information. I told you. He's one of the good guys."

"Yeah, well, Derek is one of the good guys, too."

"I never said he wasn't."

Ethan exhaled loudly. "That's good, because Derek didn't do anything and you need to find out who did."

chapter 5

"No, I don't," I said. "I'm not the police, and besides, you heard what Brady said—the police don't even know how Lewis Wallace died yet."

"Well, it's not like he had a car accident or fell down the stairs," Ethan said.

"The man could have had a heart attack or a stroke. He could have fallen and hit his head earlier in the day." I thought back to the death of Gregor Easton, which had happened when I had been in Mayville Heights for only a few months. He had died from a head injury. That case was how Marcus and I had met.

"And someone could have killed the guy," Ethan said flatly.

Hercules made a sound that might have meant he concurred or might have meant he was getting bored with the whole conversation.

"The police will figure that out." I didn't like the conversation at all.

"So can you. You've done it before."

I shook my head. "I'm not doing it this time. No."

He started to say something and I held up my hand. "No."

Anger flashed in his eyes. "So what? You want to see Derek get railroaded?"

"Do you really think Marcus would do something like that, Ethan?" I asked, my voice icy with anger. "Do you think he's that kind of person?"

Ethan ducked his head. "I wasn't saying that," he muttered.

"Good." I took a breath and let it out. "I'm not talking about this anymore," I said.

I went back into the house, trailed by Hercules. I heard the door to the backyard open and close. I figured Ethan had gone outside to either cool off or rethink his plan of attack. I hoped it wasn't the latter.

I needed to figure out what we were going to have for supper. I peered into the fridge and opened and closed cupboard doors. I had plenty of sourdough bread and enough leftover chicken to make pulled-chicken sandwiches, I decided. And a beet salad because it was fast and easy.

Hercules sat next to the refrigerator and watched me set the table, green eyes following my every move. "It's not hard to tell whose side you're on," I said the third time I passed him.

He glanced in the direction of the porch then looked at me, tipping his head to one side, which he did when he was questioning something or trying to look cute.

"We're not getting involved in this case," I said, putting a knife and fork at each place. I kept my voice low because Milo and Derek were in the living room

The cat's nose twitched.

"I mean *I'm* not getting involved in this case."

Hercules continued to stare at me.

It was really disconcerting how long he could go without blinking. "We don't even know if Lewis Wallace's death was an actual crime," I said. I set the salt and pepper shakers in the middle of the table. "And even if it was, that doesn't mean the police are seriously going to look at Derek."

The cat's green-eyed gaze never left my face.

"Why am I explaining myself to a cat?" I asked.

He almost seemed to shrug as if to say, "Darned if I know," then he yawned, stretched and headed for the living room, where I could hear the guys talking. I had a feeling the cat hadn't given up on me, either.

🐾

Susan was waiting at the bottom of the steps when I drove into the library parking lot in the morning. I parked and walked over to her. She was wearing her black cat's-eyes glasses and there were two metal straws in her updo. Susan generally wore her thick, curly hair in a topknot at work and I never quite knew what she'd use to keep it secure on any given day. Swizzle sticks, a pencil, a chopstick: It was always a surprise.

Today Susan was carrying a round metal cookie tin in addition to the tote bag holding her lunch. I looked from Susan to the can. Eric would sometimes use us as guinea pigs for whatever new recipe he had concocted. Was there one of his new recipes in that can?

"Maple sugar cookies," Susan said in answer to my unspoken question.

"You're my favorite staff member," I said as I started up the steps to unlock the front door.

She smiled. "You would probably have more credibility if I hadn't heard you say the same thing to Mary last week when she made doughnuts. But I'll take it."

She followed me inside. "I heard what your brother's friend did at The Brick Friday night." She gave me a thumbs-up. "Anyone who would kick a service dog deserves to get his as—" She looked at me. "—his assets kicked."

Her expression changed. "I also heard about the body at the St. James. It was the same guy, right? Lewis Wallace? The guy who wants—wanted—to set up his business in one of the empty warehouses?"

I nodded. "Yes, it was."

She shrugged. "I wasn't impressed with his proposal—for

one thing I think he was overestimating his profit margins—but no one should have to die alone like that." Susan headed for the stairs then. "I'll start the coffee, and then do you want me to make sure the time has changed on all the computers?"

"Please," I said. I flipped the lights on. "How do the boys handle the time change?"

"Their fiendishly computer-like brains know when it's five forty-five no matter how many times the clocks get changed," she said with a roll of her eyes. "They were making pancakes with Eric when I got up."

"That's good."

She shook her head. "No. No, really it isn't. We're going to have to paint the kitchen ceiling. Again."

It was a busy Monday at the library. Patricia Queen came in for a meeting about the upcoming quilt show. Patricia was the president of the seniors' quilting group that met every week at the library. For the last couple of years all their quilt tops had been pieced in the building before going to Patricia's home to be finished with her long-arm quilting machine. Their current project was being lap-quilted, which meant all the blocks were quilted by hand and assembled afterward. I knew the finished project would be beautiful under Patricia's exacting eye.

We sat in my office with a cup of coffee for me, and a cup of tea for Patricia, and went over the proposed schedule. I knew that some people found Patricia a bit . . . challenging to work with. She liked to plan everything down to the last detail. Mary had warned me that Patricia could be a bit obsessive but

I liked the fact that she thought of everything. I liked schedules and plans and having things well organized. As Patricia went over her proposed timeline I thought of my own mother telling my third grade teacher, "Katy likes to have all her ducks in a row. That's not a problem, is it?" in a tone that suggested that there was only one right answer to her question, which hadn't really been a question at all.

I drank the last of my coffee. "Patricia, do you think it would be possible to add a workshop of basic quilting techniques?" I asked. "I've had quite a few questions about something like that since word got out about the upcoming show."

Patricia set down her pen, nudged her wire-frame glasses up her nose and narrowed her gaze at me. "What were you thinking of?"

"Something like how to pick a design, a little color theory, how to make a basic quilt block. Just enough for people who don't know anything about quilting to get a taste of what's involved."

That was all it took for Patricia's interest to be piqued. She started listing off ideas: how the workshop could be organized, who would teach, where they could have it, etc. "I'm not sure one class would be enough," she said. "We could do one on color theory, types of blocks, fabric choice, oh, and of course how to use the rotary cutter."

"Of course," I said.

"And then another session on how to lay out the design and

sew the pieces together and a third class on constructing the quilt sandwich and doing the actual quilting."

I felt a little like I might have started a snowball of ideas rolling downhill.

Patricia had been making notes in her neat, squared-off handwriting that covered almost two pages. Finally, she looked up at me and smiled. "I'll get back to you with a plan by the end of the week."

Knowing Patricia, she'd get back to me long before Friday.

I walked her downstairs and as we got to the bottom of the steps she looked up at the beautiful carved sun Oren Kenyon had created hanging over the main entrance. It was reminiscent of the carved sun over the entrance to the first Carnegie library in Dunfermline, Scotland, with the same motto, "Let there be light," below.

"I never tire of seeing that," Patricia said. "Oren did beautiful work."

I nodded. "You're right. He's very talented."

She looked in the direction of our computer room. "How on earth did you manage to reset that clock?"

The vintage timepiece she was talking about was close to two feet wide with a heavy black circular frame and black Roman numerals on its face. I knew the clock had been in the library for at least fifty years, maybe more, although by the time the renovations began the hands had been stuck at quarter to four for several years. Although the inner workings had had to be replaced it had been important to me to keep that connection to the library's history.

"I confess that *I* didn't," I said, feeling my cheeks get pink. "Harry Taylor came in about an hour ago and did it for me."

"I always prepare for the time change by adjusting my sleeping patterns in the days before the change and by resetting my clocks early," Patricia said, with just a touch of reproach in her voice.

"I'm sure we all would benefit from doing that," I replied.

Patricia reminded me again that she would be in touch and left. I joined Mary at the checkout desk.

"Do you really think we'd all benefit from adjusting our sleeping patterns before a time change?" she asked. Her tone suggested she didn't think so.

"My alarm clock was a cat with sardine breath," I said. "I'm not exactly the best judge of that."

"You know, Patricia might benefit from learning to dance," Mary said, a sly gleam in her eyes. "Black satin and feathers flatter everyone."

Melanie Davis called midmorning. I was looking at the latest issue with our book drop. It looked like someone had hit it with a hammer or something similar. There were a couple of small dents on the top. "Remind me to show Harry," I said to Susan. "He'll be back this afternoon."

I headed up to my office to take Melanie's call, dropping

onto the edge of the desk as I reached for the phone. "How are you and how are things at the hotel?" I asked.

"Truthfully, I'm still a little shaken," she said.

"That's understandable," I said. "Finding a dead body is unsettling."

"I don't understand what Lew was doing in that meeting room. He hadn't signed up for the workshop. And the door was locked. How did he get inside?" I could hear an edge of worry in her voice.

"Maybe he was looking for you. To catch up." I picked a bit of cat hair off my sleeve. "You said you used to work together."

"We weren't exactly friends," Melanie said. "We worked together for a very short time. And anyone on staff here could have told him where to find my office." She hesitated.

I waited, not rushing to fill the silence.

Melanie sighed softly. "Back when I worked with him, Lew had a problem with insomnia. He'd be tired when he got to work because he was wandering around in the middle of the night. He told me once that his coach back in college made him go to some kind of sleep disorders clinic, but maybe he still has . . . had the problem."

I remembered what I'd read online, how Wallace had blamed his chronic insomnia for being late for football practice.

"So Mr. Wallace *was* a guest at the St. James?"

"Yes, he was," Melanie said. "The police still have his guest room and the meeting room sealed off." She sighed. "Several people have checked out and several more reservations have been canceled." She paused for a moment. "And I know it's self-ish of me to be thinking about business when a man is dead."

"It's not," I reassured her. "You still have a job to do. It's not wrong for you to do it."

"Thank you," she said. She cleared her throat. "The reason I called was *not* to complain to you. I wanted to thank you for your e-mail. And I have the answer to two of your questions."

We took a few minutes to settle a few details and agreed to reconnect hopefully later in the week.

I got a text from Ethan at about four thirty telling me that he was cooking supper. That wasn't a bad thing, but it wasn't a completely good thing, either. Ethan tended to cook more the way Maggie did, and I hoped my kitchen would survive.

When I got home Ethan was listening to one of his favorite drummers, Elvin Jones, and wearing a dishtowel tucked in at his waist as a kind of apron. The kitchen was a lot cleaner than I had expected, probably because Milo was at the sink doing dishes. "I hope you don't mind," he said, "but mess bugs me."

"No, you can't trade me for him," Ethan said from the stove. His anger at me from the night before seemed to be gone, at least for now.

I smiled at Milo. "We'll talk later," I said in a stage whisper.

Hercules and Owen were at the table, each sitting on a chair, carefully watching Ethan's every move.

I hung up my coat and bag and pulled off my boots. The kitchen smelled wonderful.

Derek wandered in from the living room. He was wearing

headphones, listening to something on his phone. He set a coffee mug on the counter next to Milo, raised one hand in hello to me and left again.

"Are you making lo mein?" I asked Ethan.

"I am," he said.

I went over to the stove and kissed the back of his head. "My favorite," I said.

Ethan held up both hands. "I live to serve."

And to suck up. He'd changed tactics, I realized. Ethan was trying to convince me to look into Lewis Wallace's death by getting on my good side. It wasn't going to work but I wasn't going to say that until I'd had a bowl of that lo mein. Or maybe two.

Ethan's cooking tasted even better than it smelled.

"I've got the dishes," Milo said. He gave me a sly grin. "And it's not up for discussion, although I will arm-wrestle you if you don't agree."

I flexed my wrist a couple of times. "If my old book-checking-out injury hadn't flared up today I think I could take you," I teased.

"How about coffee?" Ethan asked.

"Yes, if you make decaf," I said, stretching my arms up over my head. I saw Ethan send Derek a look.

"I'll make it," Derek said, getting to his feet. He gestured at the cupboard where I kept the sardine crackers and tipped his head in the direction of Owen and Hercules. "Okay if I give them each a couple?"

Two furry heads swiveled to look at me.

"Go ahead," I said. I pulled one leg up underneath me, shifting sideways in my chair. Ethan was watching me. "What?" I asked.

"Do you ever think about coming home?" he asked.

"You mean Boston."

He nodded. As usual his fingers were drumming a rhythm on the tabletop.

"Sometimes," I said. "But this is home, too. I have friends. I have a job I really like. I have those two furballs. I have Marcus. I have a life here now and I don't want to just walk away from it."

"But you have a family in Boston." His expression was serious. He wasn't teasing the way he usually did about living in the middle of nowhere with Bigfoot for a neighbor. Rebecca had laughed until tears came when I'd told her about that comment.

Ethan's visit had reminded me just how much I missed him and Sara and Mom and Dad. My stomach tied itself into a knot as I thought about how difficult it was going to be to say good-bye to him. But that didn't mean I wanted to leave behind the life I'd built in Mayville Heights. I blinked hard a couple of times. "I miss you, too," I said.

There was a knock at the door then. I got to my feet just as Marcus stepped into the room. "Hi," he said.

I smiled, closed the distance between us and gave him a quick kiss. The guys all gave some kind of acknowledgment but in Ethan's case it was a little halfhearted.

"Hi, Marcus," Derek said. "Would you like a cup of coffee? It's unleaded."

Marcus nodded. "I would, thank you."

Derek reached for a mug. Milo went back to the dishes and Ethan stayed where he was at the table, arms folded over his chest. It was the same defiant pose I remembered from when he was a teenager, which really wasn't that long ago.

"I'm glad to see you, but I thought you had another hockey practice tonight," I said.

"I do," he said. "But I needed to talk to Derek about a couple of things and I thought he might be here."

"We'll give you some privacy," I said.

Derek had poured Marcus's coffee. Now he handed him the mug. "It's okay. They can all hear whatever it is you have to say."

"Thank you," Marcus said. "Actually, all of you will probably be interested in what I came to say." He was in police officer mode, calm, logical, no emotion. "First of all, Lewis Wallace's death was not from natural causes."

"You mean he was murdered," Ethan said.

"Maybe."

"Well, which is it? Either he was murdered or he wasn't." Ethan's tone was combative.

"We're waiting for more information from the medical examiner," Marcus said.

"How did Wallace die?" I asked.

"Anaphylaxis."

Milo turned to look at us. "He was allergic to something." He wore a silver-colored Medic Alert bracelet on his right wrist warning of his own penicillin allergy.

"Yes," Marcus said. "Lewis Wallace had a peanut allergy. He'd eaten part of a peanut butter and banana muffin."

Ethan started to cough. Derek reached over and patted him on the back. Ethan held up a hand. "Sorry," he rasped. "My coffee went the wrong way."

"He ate something with peanut butter in it?" I said. "Wouldn't he have tasted it?"

Marcus had been looking at Ethan but he shifted his attention to me. "That's probably why he only had part of the muffin."

I remembered the EpiPen on the floor that at first glance I'd thought was just a regular pen. It must have belonged to Lewis Wallace.

"You said you had two things to tell Derek," I said. "What's the second?"

Marcus turned to Derek. "We know Lewis Wallace died sometime between ten p.m. Saturday night and two a.m. or so Sunday morning."

I remembered checking Wallace's body to see if he could still be alive. The timeline made sense with what I'd observed.

"We already established that you were at the bed-and-breakfast for a big chunk of that time," Marcus continued. "And we have a witness who can confirm that you were nowhere near the St. James Hotel after that."

The color drained from Derek's face. Blindly, he put a hand

out behind him and found the counter. "I uh . . . I don't under-stand," he stammered. "I told you I was just walking around."

"Someone saw you."

I touched Marcus's arm and he turned to look at me. "Who?" I said.

"Ian Queen."

"Wait a minute. Patricia Queen's son is your witness?"

Ian Queen had been in the library a couple of times, carrying boxes for the quilters. He was in his early twenties, the youngest of Patricia's children according to Mary, and a lot more laid-back than his mother. I remembered that a few months back Patricia had told me that Ian was working construction and living at home for a semester before going to graduate school in the fall. She was very proud of him.

Marcus nodded. "Ian is a credible alibi witness. He de-scribed Derek down to the jacket he was wearing." He gestured at Derek. "Ian is certain about the time and about his ID be-cause he was at The Brick Friday night. And he doesn't know you. He has absolutely no motivation to make anything up."

Ethan came around the table and gave Derek a hug, slap-ping him on the back. "This is awesome," he said. "We have to do something to celebrate." He looked at me. "Hey, Kath, what was the name of that other place you suggested?"

"Barry's Hat?" I said.

"Yeah, that was it." He looked from Derek to Milo. "What do you say? Is everybody in?"

They were. Ethan looked at me. I shook my head.

Derek turned to Marcus and extended his hand. "Thank you," he said. "I . . . I don't know what else to say."

"You're welcome," Marcus said. "I appreciate the fact that you came and talked to us. It actually helped us confirm where you were."

I smiled at Derek. "Have fun," I said. "I'm glad this is over."

He smiled back. "I will, and I promise, no getting pulled into any fights with drunks."

"Good plan," I said.

Owen had wandered in at some point and stationed himself next to the refrigerator. Ethan gestured to him. "I need to find a shirt. Come give me your opinion."

Owen dutifully followed.

Derek took his coffee cup over to the sink. Milo was telling a story that seemed to have him using that spoon I hadn't known I'd owned as a lance.

Derek wasn't a suspect. I didn't have to poke around in one of Marcus's cases and I could go back to enjoying my brother's company. All was well.

So why didn't Marcus look happier?

chapter 6

The guys left about fifteen minutes later. Apparently, Owen had chosen a dove-gray-and-dark-blue plaid shirt for Ethan. Before he headed out the door Ethan came over to Marcus. "I owe you an apology," he said. Both hands were shoved in the pockets of his dark jeans. "I kind of overreacted the first time you came to talk to Derek and again tonight. I'm sorry for being such a dick."

"You're a lot like your sister," Marcus said. "Loyal, willing to fight for the people you care about. That's not a bad thing." He glanced at me and smiled. "So don't worry about it."

They shook hands and then Ethan threw his arms around me. "Love you," he said.

"Love you more," I whispered back.

"Let's roll," Milo said. He grabbed his black down jacket and wound a long black-and-blue scarf that I recognized was one of Ella King's creations—probably bought at the co-op store—around his neck.

"Try to stay out of trouble," I said. I seemed to be saying that a lot.

"But you have bail money, right?" Milo called from the porch.

I laughed. "Just stay out of trouble, please."

Once they were gone I turned to Marcus again, catching the front of his blue ski jacket, pulling him closer so I could kiss him. "Can you stay for a few minutes?" I asked.

He nodded.

"Did you eat?"

"I had lunch." He frowned. "At least I think I did."

I gestured at the table with one finger. "Sit. I'll warm up some of Ethan's leftover lo mein."

"Your brother cooks?" Marcus asked as he shrugged off his jacket.

"We all cook," I said, going to get a bowl from the cupboard. "My mother says it's a life skill just like knowing how to swim, how to waltz and how to balance a checkbook. And by the way, he's a pretty good cook."

"Ethan's a good friend, too."

"He's not exactly subtle," I said. "I'm sorry."

Marcus draped his jacket on the back of one of the chairs,

sat down and stretched his long legs under the table. "Don't be. I meant what I said. Ethan's like you and caring about your friends isn't a bad thing. I'm just glad Ian Queen confirmed Derek's story about where he was. I have a feeling this case is going to get messy."

I got the lo mein out of the refrigerator, filled a bowl for him, and set it in the microwave. "Do you have any idea how Lewis Wallace ended up in that meeting room? He hadn't signed up for the workshop."

He raked a hand back through his dark wavy hair, a sign that he was feeling the stress. "I have no idea. There are no security cameras in that part of the hotel and so far none of the staff has admitted letting him in."

"You know that Wallace seemed to have some problem sleeping?"

Marcus nodded. "I do. And there is security footage of him wandering around other areas of the hotel. Someone from the cleaning staff asked if they could get anything for him but apparently he said he was just walking around until he was tired."

"I saw the EpiPen on the far side of the room." It had been lying on the floor against the leg of the whiteboard. Nowhere near Wallace's body.

Marcus gave me a wry smile. "I'm not surprised. You have very good observation skills."

"I'm guessing since Lewis Wallace is dead that he didn't get to use it."

"That's a good guess," he said.

"I also saw the broken glass on the floor and the overturned chair."

"I assumed you had."

"Those both suggest there was some kind of a struggle."

Marcus nodded. "They do."

The microwave beeped and I set the steaming bowl of noodles, sauce and vegetables in front of him, then got both of us fresh cups of coffee and for myself one of the remaining maple cookies from Eric that I had brought home from the library. I settled in the chair to his left, pulling one foot up underneath me. "So you don't think Wallace dropped the pen while trying to use it and then it rolled away and he knocked those things over trying to get to it?" I asked, taking a sip of my coffee.

Marcus tried a forkful of lo mein then gave a nod of approval. "That's good," he said, gesturing at the bowl with his fork. "And just between the two of us, no. The hotel building is old but it is solid and I couldn't get anything to roll that far away from where the body was."

"Someone else was in the room with him?"

He didn't say yes but he didn't say no, either.

"You're sure the muffin was the source of the peanut butter?" I broke the cookie more or less in half and took a bite. It was good, too.

Marcus reached for his own coffee. "Yes. There was a box of muffins from Sweet Thing on the table. They were peanut butter and banana. The medical examiner found part of one of those muffins in Wallace's stomach and his throat."

"The reaction must have happened very quickly if Wallace didn't even have a chance to use his EpiPen."

"Wallace had asthma. According to the medical examiner that could explain why the response was so rapid. Probably had something to do with his sleep issues." Marcus picked up his fork again. "And you've had those muffins. You really can't taste anything besides the banana. He may not have realized what he'd eaten."

"They're the ones Maggie likes so much?" I asked.

He nodded.

Out of the corner of my eye I saw Owen lick his whiskers. Georgia's peanut butter and banana muffins weren't just Maggie's favorite. They were also Owen's after half of one fell on the floor one day this past winter. The fact that it landed right in front of Owen was just a happy coincidence according to Maggie, who had actually managed to say that to me with a straight face.

"Why would a man with a severe allergy buy those muffins?" I said. "Georgia is very open about her ingredients. She doesn't make those muffins very often because they have peanut butter in them and when she does, she uses the kitchen at Fern's because the Sweet Thing kitchen is peanut-free."

Georgia shared a kitchen and workspace with the Earl of Sandwich, which ran two lunch trucks that serviced pretty much all the construction sites in the area. (And yes, the owner's name really was Earl.) They had the main floor of a two-story, blue-shingled house on Washington Street, a couple of streets above Main and two blocks east of the library. Like most of the other buildings on the street, the businesses were on the main level and there were apartments on the second floor.

Marcus shrugged. "It seems someone else bought them. Georgia is in Minneapolis for a course until the end of the week. When she gets back I'll talk to her."

I broke the last bit of my cookie in half. "Georgia isn't actually a suspect, is she?"

"No one is a suspect at the moment," he said. "We still have a lot of people to talk to."

I noticed what he'd avoided saying—that Lewis Wallace's death had been an accident. "You think Wallace was murdered," I said, watching his face closely for a reaction. I could see he was weighing his words. I waited.

"There's not much sense in denying it at this point," he said. "Yes, we do. The medical examiner is taking a bit longer than I would have liked to come to the same conclusion, but I think he'll rule Wallace's death a homicide tomorrow. Wallace did take a bite of that muffin but it looks like after that someone shoved it into his face. And there's no way his EpiPen got across the room of its own volition."

His answer confirmed what had been niggling at the back of my mind all along. "That's why you wanted to talk to Derek and why you were happy to hear he had an alibi," I said.

"Derek had more than one heated encounter with Lewis Wallace. I was glad to cross him off my list."

"Georgia had an encounter with the man." I rubbed the back of my neck. "Mayville Heights was a fresh start for her and it almost didn't work out. I don't think there's any way she could lose Emmy now, but Georgia is still skittish. Given that her in-laws tried to kidnap her child, I don't blame her."

Marcus reached across the table and caught my hand. "Don't worry. I don't think Georgia would be stupid enough to kill someone with muffins she made and then leave the box behind."

"You're right," I said.

"Look, I doubt she even sold those muffins to Lewis Wallace," he said, "but even if she did, she had no way of knowing he was allergic to peanuts."

"What about his business partners? They were going to lease some property to a group that wanted to operate a riverboat casino. Maybe they had some kind of disagreement."

He shook his head. "They were both in New York City with lots of witnesses."

Owen was still sitting between us hoping to mooch something. He gave Marcus his best plaintive kitty look. I saw Marcus glance down a couple of times at the little gray tabby.

"He's just trying to play you," I said. "Ethan has been feeding him who knows what all day."

Marcus looked down at Owen, shrugged and said, "Sorry."

The cat shot a cranky look at me, ears going in different directions. I knew that somehow he'd understood every word of the conversation.

A twist of noodle that had been wrapped around Marcus's fork slipped off just then, landing on the floor at the side of his chair. It had barely touched the floor when Owen pounced on it, quickly sniffed to make sure it was "safe" to eat and then all but slurped it up with a flick of his pink tongue. The look on his furry gray face was a mix of triumph and defiance.

I decided to let him have this one.

Marcus smiled. "I swear I didn't do that on purpose."

I smiled back at him, happy to have the subject changed. "I know you didn't. A certain little opportunistic furball has very fast reflexes." Owen straightened up, preening just a little. It seemed he took my words as a compliment.

Marcus checked the time. "I'm sorry to eat and run but I really do have to go." He got to his feet. "Thank you for supper."

I got to my feet as well and he pulled me close for a kiss that led to a second kiss.

We broke apart very reluctantly. "I really do have to meet Eddie," Marcus said.

I grabbed my jacket. "I know," I said. "I'll walk you out."

The sky was an endless inky black pierced with brilliant stars overhead. Marcus put an arm around me. I leaned into him and I was anything but cold.

His SUV was parked behind my truck. And there was a small ginger tabby cat standing on her hind legs, looking out of the driver's window.

Micah.

Marcus stopped in his tracks. He stared at the car. "How the hell did she get in there?" he said. "I swear I checked the backseat. She wasn't there. This doesn't make any sense."

I opened my mouth to explain, and then closed it again. Marcus was in the middle of a murder investigation. This wasn't the time. It really wasn't.

His cat seemingly appearing out of nowhere in Marcus's car did make sense to me. The little ginger tabby—who was missing the tip of her tail—was also a Wisteria Hill cat, although she didn't share Owen's and Hercules's dislike of being touched by most people. She did, however, share Owen's ability to disappear. I really didn't understand how she'd evaded being caught at it by Marcus for so long other than she was a very intelligent cat. Like Owen and Hercules, it certainly seemed as though she understood everything that was said around her.

Marcus shook his head slowly, still staring at the SUV. "I feel like I'm losing my mind sometimes."

I snaked one arm around his midsection and gave him a squeeze. "You're not," I said.

"She's snuck into the car twice in the last two days," he said. "No. Make that three times now." He exhaled loudly, his breath lingering for a moment in the night air. "The second time I was halfway to work before I saw her in the rearview mirror sitting in the middle of the backseat. I don't know how the heck I missed her before that and I have no idea how she got past me into the car in the first place. I have no idea how she got in tonight."

My chest tightened as though I'd been picked up and hugged by King Kong. "She is small and . . . fast," I said, wondering if I sounded as lame to him as I sounded to myself.

Micah was watching us out the window of the SUV, her head cocked to one side as though she was trying to figure out what we were talking about.

Marcus shook his head again. "I've gotta start paying better attention. It's too cold for her to be stuck in the car for so long."

"You've only been here for about half an hour," I said. "And Micah lived outside before she lived with you. I think she's all right."

"I'll start checking under the seats," he said. "She's so little she can fit in some pretty small spaces, and you're right about her being fast. This morning, for a moment, I actually thought she had disappeared right in front of me." He gave me a sheepish grin. "I guess that's what happens when I don't get enough sleep or enough caffeine."

Or when your cat has some kind of unexplained magical ability.

Marcus opened the SUV's door and picked up the little cat. I reached over to stroke her fur and she nuzzled my hand. "No more sneaking into the car," I said.

Micah gave me the same unblinking look Owen liked to use when he was ignoring me.

I gave her one last scratch behind her right ear and Marcus set her back on the seat again. He wrapped both arms around me and kissed me again. And then again. I could have stood there all night. I wasn't the slightest bit cold.

Marcus rested his chin on the top of my head and groaned. "I have to stop doing this or I'm never going to get out of here and Eddie is going to string me up."

I broke out of his embrace and took two steps backward, folding my hands neatly in front of me.

"That doesn't help at all," he said.

I gave him a teasing smile. "What? I'm just standing here minding my manners."

"More like taking my breath away." He shook his head. "I'm going now. I'll talk to you tomorrow." He slid onto the seat, started the SUV and backed out of the driveway.

I gave a little wave and he was gone. All of a sudden I was cold. I wrapped my coat around me and hurried around the side of the house.

When I stepped into the kitchen I found Owen sitting in Marcus's seat.

"You seem to have forgotten that the chairs are for people," I said.

He gave a pointed look at the door and then shifted his gaze to me again, giving a sharp, insistent meow as though he somehow knew what had just occurred out in the driveway. For all I knew, he did.

I put a hand on my hip. "What was I supposed to do? Say 'Yes, you actually did see Micah disappear because, oh, I forgot to mention she can do that kind of thing'?"

Being a cat of few words, he just continued to silently eye me. It was very disconcerting.

I reached down, picked Owen up and took his seat, setting him on my lap. I remembered when I'd first begun to suspect Owen and his brother had some unexplainable abilities. In Owen's case the idea had begun to take form after he'd ended up at the library and had launched himself onto someone's head. The someone was conductor Gregor Easton, who'd had no sense of humor about that sort of thing.

I remembered how Susan had laughed once the pompous conductor had been placated and Owen had been corralled in my office.

"Suddenly, there he was on the maestro's head," she'd said, shoulders shaking with laughter. "It was almost like one second he was invisible and the next he wasn't."

Luckily the phone had started to ring then, which had ended the conversation. I'd wondered what Susan would have said if I had told her that I thought it was possible the cat actually *had* vanished for a moment.

That incident wasn't the first time I thought I'd seen Owen disappear. That had happened six weeks prior. I'd been in the swing in the backyard with Owen on the grass at my feet watching the birds. And then he wasn't. I looked for him, certain he'd darted away to stalk some unsuspecting robin. Then he appeared again, about ten feet away in midair, in midleap over a tiny black-and-yellow finch.

"Owen!" I'd yelled. The bird flew away, I lost my balance

and tumbled onto the lawn, and the cat landed on the grass, legs splayed, looking very undignified. As I settled on the swing again I'd decided I hadn't really seen Owen disappear and then reappear. The sun had been in my eyes. My mind had been wandering. And then he did it again.

Was I having a breakdown, I'd wondered, or maybe a very bizarre hallucination?

I'd gotten up, walked across the grass and sat down next to the cat. "Owen, do that again," I'd said.

He'd stared at me.

"C'mon. Disappear." I'm not sure what I had been expecting, maybe some sort of slow fade-out, the way *Alice in Wonderland*'s Cheshire cat had disappeared, until only its smile was left. Owen looked at me like I'd lost my mind. And then he disappeared. Except this time he'd only disappeared behind the red chokeberry bush.

I'd learned about Hercules's abilities at the library as well, back when it was being renovated. I was shutting things down for the night when the little tuxedo cat decided to explore one of the partially finished meeting rooms. When I bent to scoop him up he darted away.

"Hercules, come back here right now," I'd said sharply. In return all I'd gotten was a low, rumbly meow. He had walked out of my reach, through the closed panel door in front of us, and disappeared.

I remembered how my knees had started to shake. I sat down hard on the floor. Hercules had vanished. He hadn't darted past me. He'd walked through a solid wooden door just as though it wasn't there and it was almost as though there was a faint "pop" as the end of his tail had disappeared. I'd felt all over the door looking for some kind of hidden panel but the door was thick and unyielding.

I'd sat back on my heels, wondering if I was crazy. I'd remembered a psych prof in freshman year telling the class that if you could ask the question then you weren't. Of course, three-quarters of the time he came to class in his pajama bottoms.

I'd pressed my head to my knees and made myself take several shaky breaths. No climbing on the crazy bus, I'd told myself. I was tired. I needed glasses. There was a rational explanation for all of this.

Maybe five minutes went by, although it had seemed a lot longer. Then I had felt . . . something I couldn't define. It was as though the air around the door suddenly thickened and pushed against me the way water pushes against your hand if you try to press it over the end of a hose. And Hercules had walked through the door as though there wasn't any door there at all.

It defied the laws of physics. It couldn't have happened.

Except it had.

I didn't know what to do. I knew I couldn't tell the truth— not that I was even sure what the truth was. And so I'd kept the secret for three years. I'd kept it from Roma and Maggie and Rebecca. From my mother and Ethan.

I'd kept it from Marcus. I knew I couldn't do that much longer.

chapter 7

The next few days were uneventful. On Tuesday, Ethan, Derek and Milo went to see the luthier in Red Wing. I knew that a luthier was someone who repaired and built guitars, but Milo explained, over a bowl of oatmeal and applesauce, that they did a lot more than that.

"They don't just work on guitars, they work on all sorts of stringed wooden instruments—guitars, violins, violas, cellos, double basses," he said. "And they build instruments, too."

The three of them came back from Red Wing enthused about the woman and her workshop. They had left Milo's old guitar with her and she had promised it would be ready by the time they had to leave.

Maggie had invited the guys to join our tai chi class. Derek had turned down the offer to do more work on his song. Ethan, of course, had accepted. To my surprise Milo had decided to join us, too.

The three of us squeezed into my truck and drove down the hill.

"How long have you been doing tai chi?" Milo asked.

"About three years," I said. "Rebecca invited me to try a class and I liked it. I've been going ever since. My balance is better. I'm more aware of how my body moves. When we do the form at the end of the class it's very much like meditating."

"The form?" Ethan said.

I nodded. "Maggie teaches Wu style tai chi chuan. There are one hundred and eight movements. Those movements make up the form. You'll see once we get started."

I stopped to let two people and a shaggy sheep dog cross the street.

"You said Maggie teaches Wu style," Milo said. "So does that mean there are other styles?"

"There are five major styles," I said. "Chen, Yang, Wu Hao, Wu and Sun. Chen style dates all the way back to the sixteenth century. There are other hybrids and offshoots now, but those are the main ones."

"So you've learned all one hundred and whatever of the movements?" Ethan said.

I nodded. "Uh-huh." I remembered when that had seemed impossible.

"Then why do you keep going?"

"Because there're always parts of the form that can be improved." I thought of my nemesis, Cloud Hands. "Because I like the people. Because there are new things to learn." I smiled. "Because it's fun. You'll see."

I found a parking spot close to the studio and the guys followed me up the stairs to the studio. We hung up our jackets and I sat down to change my shoes. Something about the door seemed to have caught Milo's attention.

"Is there something wrong with that door?" I asked.

"Not the door, the lockset," he said. The door was original to the old building, I knew, and had round brass doorknobs that I assumed were also original.

Maggie had seen the three of us and walked over. "Hi," she said. "Is there a problem?"

"You know this door isn't very secure, right?" Milo said.

Her green eyes narrowed. "No, what's wrong with it?"

Milo held up a finger. "Watch this." He closed the door and set the lock. Then he took out his wallet and pulled out a card. It was thin enough to slide between the door and the frame. I watched him maneuver it for a moment and the door swung open. He grinned and held up the plastic rectangle. "And you thought this was just a library card."

"How did you do that?" Maggie asked.

Milo closed and locked the door again and handed his library card to Maggie. With his coaching she got the door open. It took her a little more time than it had taken him. But not much.

I had noticed similar setups in other older buildings in town, including at one time, the library. I reminded myself to thank Harry Junior for insisting on replacing all of the old locksets at the library.

"How did you know this?" I asked.

"He's a *Dateline* fanatic," Ethan said. "We watch it quite a lot between sets when we're playing somewhere."

"You'd be surprised what you can learn from that show," Milo added.

Ethan looked at Maggie. "We can put a deadbolt on that door for you. I mean, if you want one."

Maggie nodded. "I do."

The three of them headed for the tea table, talking about what would be the best choice for the old door.

After class we headed down to Eric's for chocolate pudding cake. Maggie shared the story of the time we'd found what we thought was a dead rat floating in the co-op store's flooded basement and how I'd fished it out and tossed what I thought was a rodent corpse into the street and instead launched a very alive rat at Ruby. Ethan laughed so hard coffee came out his nose.

Melanie Davis and I managed to squeeze in a quick meeting Wednesday afternoon to go over the last few details we had to coordinate for the quilt show.

Her office was small and cramped and didn't even have a

window. There was a desk, a locked credenza for files, a couple of chairs and a small lamp. A woven scarlet-and-gray blanket was draped over the arm of one of the chairs. There was a calendar on the wall along with a beautiful photo of the River-walk that I recognized as Ruby's work and a tiny plaque with the words "Valor, Truth, Honor."

"Sorry for the cramped surroundings," Melanie said. "This is just a temporary space for me." She pointed over her head. "The offices and two washrooms upstairs are being renovated, so for now, I'm here."

I found the room a little claustrophobic and wondered if maybe Melanie did, too, and that was why her door wasn't just wide open, it was being held that way by a wooden wedge.

"This room was originally the bottom of a ventilation shaft," she said.

I looked around. "That explains why there are no windows."

She pointed to the ornate brass grill covering a large opening on the wall. It was the most striking feature in the room. "It's not original, it's a replica, but the heating and air-conditioning vents will all have grates like that in the new offices. It's a way to keep a little history of the building."

Melanie indicated the open door. "All the stone and concrete in here interfere with my cell phone. I have to keep the door open to get any signal. Sometimes I'm hanging over the front of the desk with the phone, trying to make a call." She shook her head. "And Murphy's Law in action I guess, the phone company is running new lines in this part of the building so some days I have a landline and some I don't. In other words, if you need to get in touch with me, I suggest carrier pigeon."

"I was thinking I could tie a note to Owen's leg and send him over," I said.

Melanie smiled. "That would work, too." She glanced at her cell phone. "Seriously, if you can't get me on my cell you can leave a message at the front desk."

"I will," I said. I looked around the small room. "What will happen to this space?"

"It'll most likely be used for storage," Melanie said. She gestured at the opening in the wall. "And that will be bricked off."

I felt an involuntary shiver like a cold finger trailing up my spine. I didn't do well in small spaces.

It didn't take long for us to go over the last few details for the quilt show. I was glad to be able to cross that off of my to-do list.

"Thanks for fitting me into your schedule, Kathleen," Melanie said as she walked me back out to the front desk from her office after we finished. She was wearing a deep green blouse and a slim chocolate skirt and she looked like an early promise of spring. "Patricia's called me three times in the last two days."

"She's a very detail-oriented person," I said.

Melanie smiled. "And you're very diplomatic."

We passed the hallway that led to the meeting room where we'd found Lewis Wallace's body.

"We got both rooms back yesterday," Melanie said. "I admit I felt a little . . . unsettled walking into that meeting room."

"That's understandable," I said.

"It wasn't technically my first dead body," she continued. "I worked in a hotel in Vermont and we had a guest pass away in his sleep, but in that case he was a hundred and two and it just didn't seem as . . ." She paused. "It was sad, of course, but not as much of a shock as finding the body of someone you"—she cleared her throat—"someone you used to know, someone you didn't expect to see dead."

I nodded. "I know what you mean." We passed a waiter pushing a wheeled food cart. He smiled at both of us. "Did Lewis Wallace have any family?" I asked.

Melanie shook her head. "He was an only child and his parents died when he was just in college." She bent down to pick up a crumpled gum wrapper from the carpet. "I remember hearing something about a brief marriage when he was playing football in Canada but I don't know if that was even true. He supposedly made a bunch of money up there."

We stepped out into the lobby. "Is what happened still affecting business here?" I asked.

Melanie shook her head. "Umm, no. After those first few early checkouts and cancellations things went back to normal. I guess people have short memories."

"I'm glad to hear that," I said. "If there's anything else you need, please let me know."

She thanked me again and I headed back to the library.

Ruby had convinced all three guys to come talk to the Reading Buddies kids about music and songwriting after school on Wednesday. We set up a couple of big whiteboards and to my surprise they actually managed to write an entire song with the kids' help. Hearing the guitar music ring through the library—which Ethan said had very good acoustics—when I stepped back inside the building after my meeting made me feel a little homesick remembering all the times over the years that I'd heard Ethan playing at home.

Thursday morning I had a meeting with Patricia Queen and Oren Kenyon to finalize all the details for the displays planned for the library during the quilt show. Oren Kenyon was a jack-of-all-trades. He'd worked on the library renovation and the repairs to the Stratton Theatre. If you could explain what you wanted to Oren he could build it. He was also a very talented musician.

Our meeting was scheduled for ten thirty and Patricia walked into the building at exactly twenty-five minutes after. Oren had already arrived and was standing in the computer area looking up at the ceiling at the system of fine wires and pulleys we had used in the past to display everything from artwork to old photographs to flying ghosts at Halloween.

Patricia had drawn a sketch of the main floor of the library as well as a detailed floor plan to scale. There were quilts to display—new and vintage—as well as books and magazines on the subject and a collection of photos of the group taken over the years. A tiny color-coded key on the side of her floor plan showed where everything should go. She handed the drawing to Oren and he studied it for a moment, nodding slowly as a hint of a smile spread across his face. "This is excellent, Patricia," he said. He looked at me. "Kathleen, what do you think?"

I pointed at one tiny blue square. "Will this"—I squinted at the key—"quilt be too close to the heating vent?"

Patricia's head came up and her eyes darted from side to side. "That's one of our vintage quilts," she said. "It's over a hundred years old." She reminded me of a groundhog coming out of its burrow, looking around trying to decide if we were getting six more weeks of winter.

"I'll show you the vent Kathleen is talking about," Oren said. He gestured in the direction of the magazines section and gave me a small smile as he passed in front of me. It occurred to me that if anyone was diplomatic, it was Oren.

Much like his son, Oren's father, Karl, had been good with his hands. But what he had really wanted to be was an artist. He had created some incredible sculptures. The moment I'd seen them in Oren's workshop I'd known they deserved to be seen and appreciated. I'd convinced Oren to let me display some of his father's pieces here at the library. That had been the beginning of several shows and Karl Kenyon had finally gotten the acclaim he should have gotten when he was alive. It had cemented the friendship between Oren and me.

Moving that one quilt turned out to be the only change that was needed to Patricia's plan. She seemed happy with Oren's suggestions for suspending the quilts from the ceiling so they could be seen but not handled. "There are just too many grubby little hands in here in the run of a day," she said. "No offense, Kathleen," she added.

"None taken," I said. I felt sure Patricia would have been appalled to see what some of those grubby little hands did to our library books.

"Thank you," I said to Oren after Patricia left. "We wouldn't be able to do this without your help. If we couldn't hang the quilts they wouldn't be safe from little hands and big ones, too."

Oren ducked his head. "You're welcome. I'm happy I can help."

"Is there anything you need?" I asked.

He looked up at me. "Would you mind if I checked the hooks in the computer area? I noticed one that doesn't look quite right."

I smiled. "Go ahead."

Oren headed to the loading dock to get the tall stepladder.

I picked up my notepad and the folder of papers Patricia had given me and turned around just as Georgia Tepper walked into the building. So she was back in town from her workshop. I wondered if Marcus knew.

Georgia looked around, smiling when she spotted me.

I walked over to join her. "Hi," I said. "How was the workshop?"

Her smile got even bigger. "It was wonderful. I think I'm still on a sugar high."

She was holding her cell phone in one hand. I gestured at it. "Any pictures to share?"

Her gaze slipped away from mine for a moment. I'd noticed she sometimes tended to downplay her skills. "Yes," she finally said.

I waited while she scrolled through her photos. Then she held out the phone to me.

"Oh, Georgia, that's beautiful!" I exclaimed. The cake pictured on the screen was a four-tiered creation with alternating black and white layers decorated with a curving cascade of flowers from pale violet to dark purple down the front. "It's almost too pretty to eat."

She smiled again. "Thank you for saying that."

"I can't resist asking; what kind of cake? Chocolate and vanilla?"

"Close," she said. "The dark layers are dark chocolate and the light layers are hazelnut."

"That's even better," I said. "You're really talented." I looked at the screen a second time "Those flowers, they look so real."

"They're not hard to make," she said, swiping her index finger across the phone screen to show me a closer image of the delicate blooms. "I could teach you, I mean, if you're interested."

I nodded. "Yes. I'm absolutely interested. As soon as the quilt show is over I'll have some free time."

"We'll set up a time then." She tucked her phone in the pocket of her jacket. "The quilt show is actually the reason I'm here. Patricia Queen sent me an e-mail—well, several e-mails—while I was out of town."

"She wants the show to be perfect," I said. I knew some

people found Patricia's dogged attention to detail annoying, but I admired her work ethic.

"I understand that," Georgia said. "I can be pretty single-minded myself when I'm baking. It turns out Patricia wants one of my gift baskets as a thank-you gift for Melanie Davis but she couldn't give me any ideas about what to put in it. I don't want to deliver a basket of, say, banana muffins, if what Melanie would really enjoy is chocolate cupcakes."

"Chocolate cupcakes, definitely," I said at once. I knew that Melanie loved chocolate. She'd asked for the recipe after she tried one of my brownies. And I was positive that she wouldn't feel like banana muffins—or any other kind of muffin—at the moment.

Georgia scrolled through her phone once again and showed me some of the cupcake possibilities. I'd tried all of them, I realized.

"They all look so delicious," I said, "and I know how good they taste, but I think Melanie would like the mix of double chocolate, mint chocolate chip and mocha fudge." Just looking at a picture of those cupcakes made me hungry, and right on cue my stomach growled. Loudly.

I put a hand on my midsection. "Sorry," I said, feeling my cheeks get red with embarrassment.

Georgia laughed. "Don't apologize. I take that as praise." She tucked her phone in her pocket again. "By the way, was your brother happy with his muffins?"

His muffins?

I gave her a blank look. "I'm sorry, what muffins are we talking about?"

"The peanut butter banana ones I made for the workshop he was teaching on Sunday."

"Ethan ordered peanut butter banana muffins from you? For the songwriting workshop at the hotel?" I knew I was parroting her words but I couldn't help it. I was trying to have them make sense because they didn't at the moment.

Georgia frowned. "Kathleen, was there something wrong with them?" she asked.

"No, no," I said. "It's just that the workshop was canceled. You probably didn't hear because you left early on Sunday morning."

"Yes," she said, still looking very confused.

How was I going to explain this? "A guest at the hotel . . . died."

She put a hand to her chest. "That's horrible!" she whispered.

I exhaled softly. "There's something else you should know. That guest was, uh, Lewis Wallace."

Georgia stared wide-eyed at me. "Oh my word. You mean the man from Fern's who . . . who . . ." She didn't finish the sentence.

"Yes," I said.

"What happened?"

I hesitated for a moment. I couldn't bring myself to say he was murdered and I didn't think Marcus would want me to say anything at this point, anyway. "The police are still investigating but it looks as though he died from an allergic re-action." I hoped she wouldn't make the connection, but she did.

The color drained from her face. "An allergic reaction? What? To the peanut butter? Do you mean— Did I kill the man?"

"No!" I said, vehemently shaking my head. "You had noth-ing to do with Lewis Wallace's death. Absolutely nothing." I reached out and gave her arm a squeeze. "Talk to Marcus, Georgia. He'll tell you the same thing. Please."

She nodded. "I . . . I think I'll do that." She patted the pocket that held her phone. "I'm sorry. I need to get going. Thanks for your help, Kathleen."

"If I can do anything else—anything—please call me or stop in."

"I will," she said. She raised a hand in good-bye and headed out.

I folded my arms over my chest and blew out a breath. My stomach felt as though a troupe of circus acrobats were doing a tumbling routine in there.

Ethan ordered those muffins.

Ethan.

Why hadn't he said so?

chapter 8

I thought about texting Ethan or even calling him, but I decided not to. He was doing another song-writing workshop with a Boys and Girls Club in Red Wing and I didn't want to disrupt that. And I wanted to see his face when I asked him what the heck he'd been thinking. I kept telling myself that he had to have had a good reason for not mentioning to Marcus or to me that he'd bought the muffins that had caused Lewis Wallace's allergic reaction. I just couldn't come up with one.

I ate the last of the lo mein for supper, grateful that Ethan had made lots of it. Owen kept me company while I washed the dishes, going through his own elaborate personal hygiene routine.

My thoughts kept going back to what I'd learned from Georgia. That's all that I'd been able to think about since she'd stopped by the library. "Why did Ethan order those muffins and why didn't he say anything?" I said, more to myself than to the cat. "And how did they get to the hotel?"

"Merow!" Owen said loudly.

I turned to find him eyeing me, one paw hovering in the air and what to me seemed like a confused expression in his golden eyes. At the same time Hercules came in from the porch, stopped halfway across the kitchen floor and looked from his brother to me. "Mrr," he said as though he was asking what he'd just missed.

I gestured to his food and water dishes by the refrigerator. "You missed supper."

He glanced over at his food but his gaze came back to Owen. They stared silently at each other in that way that once again made me think that they somehow had the ability to communicate without making a sound. Finally, Hercules looked at me and gave a soft murp while Owen went back to meticulously washing his face.

It really did seem as though Hercules had been asking what I'd been talking about and I knew it would help me sort out my thoughts as well as work out what I was going to say to my brother if I talked to the cats.

"Ethan bought those muffins," I said. "He knew that Lewis Wallace had died from an allergic reaction. Marcus even said the man had eaten a peanut butter and banana muffin."

I remembered how Ethan had started to cough and said it was because his coffee had gone down the wrong way.

I pointed a fork in the cats' direction and drops of water spattered onto the floor. "The little weasel must have gotten them to the hotel somehow. They weren't here in the house."

Owen gave a very enthusiastic meow. "Yes, I know they're your favorite," I said, setting a bowl in the dish rack to drain. "That's because they're Maggie's favorite."

Hercules had come to sit beside me. The cats looked at each other again then they both fixed their kitty gazes on me. I felt as though I was missing something. Along with a delicious selection of cupcakes, Georgia offered a few muffin choices: banana chocolate chip—my favorite—blueberry, apple spice and peanut butter banana—Owen and Maggie's favorite.

Maggie.

I dropped the glass I was washing back into the soapy water and leaned against the counter. "He bought those muffins for Maggie, didn't he? Ruby convinced her to sign up for the workshop." I had noticed the way Ethan had smiled at Mags, how he'd grinned with pleasure when she'd complimented his singing, how he'd referred to Brady as *her boyfriend or whatever he was.* I wasn't wrong about him having a crush on her.

"He probably picked them up from Georgia and dropped them off at the hotel before they went out that Saturday night." Which was something Marcus needed to know, I realized. It could possibly help him tighten up the timeline.

"But how did Ethan know peanut butter and banana

SOFIE KELLY

muffins were Maggie's favorite?" I asked Hercules. As soon as I said the words out loud I knew the answer. "That was me. I gave him that muffin for her from the batch Abigail brought to the library, the day we had lunch at Eric's. That's how Ethan knew they were her favorite." I blew out a breath. "Crap on toast."

Hercules's whiskers twitched. I took that as an indication that he agreed with me.

"He definitely has a big crush on her," I said, reaching for the dishcloth. "And he didn't want me to know. That's why he didn't say anything. Still, he should have said something to Marcus."

Hercules was already on the way to his dishes. He gave a flick of his tail. I knew the cat version of "Duh" when I saw it.

"No wonder I couldn't come up with a reason for Ethan to keep his mouth shut. I was looking for a good reason, not a lame one."

Owen gave a murp of agreement and started washing his tail.

I checked the time and realized I could make it to tai chi. I had just enough time to change and get down the hill. It would be a while before Ethan got back. I knew going to class was a better use of my time than wandering around the house grumbling about Ethan to the cats.

When I got out of my truck Simon Janes was waiting on the sidewalk for me. Simon was the father of Mia, my former intern. He was also my friend. At least I hoped he still thought of

140

me as a friend. Simon had wanted more than that and maybe if I'd never met Marcus . . . but I had.

Mia's mother had died when she was born and Simon had raised her with the help of his father. She and I had gotten close in the time she'd worked for me, especially after her grandfather was murdered. That close relationship hadn't diminished when she'd gone away to college.

Simon smiled when he caught sight of me. "Hi," he said. He was wearing jeans and a fitted navy down jacket. "I was hoping I hadn't missed you."

Simon was tall with a rangy build and hair buzzed close to his scalp. He had a crescent-shaped scar that ran from the end of his right eyebrow to just below the eye.

"I was out of town on business and stopped to see Mia. She sent this for you." He handed over a small brown paper shopping bag. The handles were tied together with a pink ribbon.

Inside the bag was a folded black T-shirt.

"Mia said you'd get it."

I unfolded the shirt and laughed. I held it up so he could see. Across the front was my favorite Groucho Marx line: *Outside of a dog, a book is man's best friend. Inside of a dog, it's too dark to read.*

Simon smiled.

"Thank you for bringing this," I said. "I'll call Mia as soon as I get home."

"She'd like that." He studied me for a moment, hands stuffed in the pockets of his jacket. "How have you been?"

"Busy. My brother and two of his friends are here." I hesitated for a moment. "How are you?"

"You know me," he said with a self-deprecating smile. "Eat. Sleep. Work. Repeat."

"Maybe you could add fun to that list," I said.

He nodded. "Maybe I could."

He said good night then and walked away down the sidewalk.

When I got upstairs I found Rebecca changing her shoes.

It occurred to me that she and Everett might be able to tell me more about Lewis Wallace's proposed business and maybe even a little about the man.

I sat down next to her. "Hello, my dear," she said. "How are you?" She had a gorgeous smile. No wonder Everett had been in love with her for basically his entire life.

"I'm well, thank you," I said. "Is Everett back from his trip?"

She leaned down to tuck her boots under the bench. "He is."

"Could I come by for a minute in the morning? I'd like to talk to both of you about something."

"You're welcome anytime," she said, patting my arm. "You know we're early birds so just walk over when it works for you."

I thanked her and said that I would. Roma came up the stairs then and that was the end of the conversation.

When I got home I settled into the big chair in the living room with a lap full of cat and called Mia to thank her for the shirt. We talked for half an hour. I could tell she was doing well and that she was happy. That made me happy, too.

I was at the table working on staffing schedules on my laptop when Ethan came through the back door. I could feel the energy coming off of him. He was in a great mood. "Hey, Kath," he said. "Oh man, you should have been there. The kids were great. They all know so much about music—which bands and artists are hot, what the trends are. The questions? I feel like my brain got a workout. And they're all so creative. You wouldn't believe what they came up with for lyrics and music." He finally seemed to realize I hadn't said a word. "What's up?" he asked.

My arms crossed over my chest. "You need to talk to Marcus," I said.

"Sure." He opened the fridge and looked inside, frowning at the contents. "You know what he wants?"

I got to my feet. "I didn't say he needs to talk to you. *You* need to talk to him."

He shrugged. "Okay. And what do I *need* to talk to him about?" His tone was flippant.

"You need to tell him that you were the one who bought those muffins that Lewis Wallace had the allergic reaction to."

Ethan straightened up, shut the refrigerator door and turned to face me. There were two bright spots of color high on his cheekbones. "What makes you think that?"

I leaned forward and snapped the side of his head with my thumb and index finger. "I talked to Georgia. She asked me how you liked the muffins you ordered from her for the song-writing workshop. That's what makes me think that."

His mouth moved and I waited for him to start arguing with me. Instead he gave me a long look and said, "Butt out of my life, Kathleen."

"Excuse me?" I said.

"You heard me." His voice was surprisingly even and controlled. "This is none of your business."

"It is my business," I retorted. My voice, in contrast, sounded harsh and loud. "Marcus needs to know that you're the one who bought those muffins and it should be you who tells him, not me." I folded my arms over my chest again and glared at him.

"Who says he doesn't?" he said.

I stared at him. "What do you mean?"

"Who says that Marcus doesn't know that I bought them?"

"So you did tell him?" I said. "You didn't say anything to me."

His chin came up. "No, I didn't tell you," Ethan said. "That doesn't mean that I didn't say anything to Marcus. Give me a little credit, Kath. I'm not stupid."

For a moment I truly didn't know what to say. "I don't understand," I finally managed to mumble.

"No, you don't," Ethan replied, a little aggravation in his voice now. "You treat me like I'm still running around in footie pajamas, Kath. I have a mother. I don't need another one."

I looked at him and suddenly all I could see was baby Ethan

with his hair going every which way just like it was now, smiling and holding up his arms as I reached to lift him out of his crib in the middle of the night so we could watch cheesy late movies on TV. I'd always been more than just an older sibling with Ethan and Sara and not just because of the age difference between us. Because our mom and dad were actors and could get very caught up in whichever characters they were creating, sometimes it had seemed like I was the only adult in the house.

A lump of guilt knotted in my chest. "I'm sorry," I said. I knew better than anyone what Mom could be like when she wanted details on some part of our lives. I'd been getting that kind of third degree for longer than Ethan had. No wonder he didn't tell me that he had a bit of a crush on Maggie, or anything else for that matter.

"Look, I get that you want to take care of me," he said. "But I swear I can take care of myself. I shave. I pay taxes. I eat my vegetables—most of the time." A hint of a smile flashed across his face.

"I know that," I said, fighting the urge to reach over and smooth down a particularly wayward clump of his hair. "You're smart. You're talented. You're funny."

He made a "keep going" gesture with one hand. "You don't have to stop."

I smiled at him. "I really am sorry."

He nodded. "I get that, Kath." He leaned back against the refrigerator. "You get that I had nothing to do with that man's death, right?"

"Of course I do," I said.

"Milo wanted to wash his hair before we went out that night. You know how obsessive he is about it. The guy brought three bottles of conditioner with him. So I dropped him and Derek off at the place where they're staying and told them I'd be back. I went and picked up the muffins and I left them in the meeting room. That's it. I didn't see Wallace."

I held up one hand. "Hang on a second. How did you get into the room? That door should have been locked."

He shrugged and gave me a sly smile. "I'm cute."

I sighed. "You charmed some woman into letting you into that meeting room, didn't you?"

"Front desk clerk. I just wanted to leave the muffins there. I knew if I brought them home you'd ask me a whole bunch of questions." He narrowed his gaze at me. "And I don't want her to get in trouble or fired for that, by the way."

"You bought them for Maggie, didn't you?" I said.

"Yes, I bought them for Maggie," he said. He at least had the good grace to blush. "Now do I get the speech that she's your friend and she's too old for me?"

I shook my head. "Nope."

He narrowed his gaze at me. "Seriously?"

"Seriously."

"But I had a whole thing about how wrong you are," he said.

"You don't need it," I said. "Like you said, you're a grown

man, not a little kid. I promise I'll try harder not to cramp your style, as they say."

Ethan rolled his eyes. "Nobody says that, Kath."

I kissed his cheek. "Love you," I said. I picked up my computer and headed for the stairs.

"Love you, too," he called after me.

Hercules was in my bedroom. The closet door was partway open and he was nudging one of my black flats across the floor. He made a face and his tail whipped across the floor when I bent down and picked up the shoe. It was the third time I'd caught him doing the same thing.

"Why do you keep taking my shoe out of the closet?" I asked. He looked from the black flat to me, his green gaze steady and unblinking. I wasn't sure if he had some nefarious purpose for trying to swipe my footwear or he was making a statement about my fashion choices. Given how vocal he could be when I was getting dressed, I kind of suspected the latter.

I put the shoe back in the closet, then bent down and picked up the little tuxedo cat. "Ethan came clean to Marcus," I told him. "It was just me that he didn't tell about buying those muffins." I didn't add that was because I was a bossy, interfering big sister. Hercules licked my chin, which might have been a gesture of comfort or might have been because I had a bit of lo mein sauce on my face.

I knew Marcus didn't suspect Ethan. He didn't know Lewis Wallace, and other than the incident when he and Derek ran into the man on the sidewalk outside Eric's Place, Ethan had never spoken to him. No one would seriously think of him as a suspect. But he was my baby brother and I was a little—or from his perspective, more than a little—overprotective.

"We have to figure out who killed Lewis Wallace," I said.

"Mrr," Hercules agreed. He put one white-tipped paw on my hand. He was in.

chapter 9

When Rebecca let me into her kitchen the next morning I discovered that Hercules was already there, sitting on a chair next to Everett at the table, a couple of organic fish crackers on a napkin in front of him.

"Rebecca, why is my cat at your breakfast table?" I asked.

"It's Friday," she said, picking up a heavy brown stoneware mug from the counter and making her way over to the coffeepot.

"I'm aware of what day it is," I said.

"Hercules has breakfast with Everett on Tuesdays and Fridays. Where else would he be sitting, dear? On the floor?"

There was something about Rebecca, maybe it was her

innate kindness, that made people care about her, that made them—me included—just a little protective, at which, for the most part, Rebecca just smiled. On the other hand, underneath that gray hair and angelic smile there was a steel-hard stubborn streak.

Hercules having a place at her table sounded so perfectly logical that I knew better than to argue with her. I saw a hint of a smile on Everett's face but he just picked up his own coffee cup and didn't say a word.

Rebecca set the steaming mug in front of me. "Thank you," I said, reaching for the blue cut-glass sugar bowl.

"Have you had breakfast?" she asked.

I nodded. "I have. Coffee is fine."

"Well if you change your mind I have fruit and yogurt and cinnamon raisin bread." She smiled. "I wanted to tell you that I heard about that unpleasant incident at The Brick last week and while I don't generally condone violence, I don't care for bullies, especially people who mistreat animals and don't show respect for our veterans. I would have reacted just the way your friend did. I hope there haven't been any repercussions for him."

I shook my head. "There haven't. And for the record, Derek is a good guy. He doesn't go around getting into altercations in bars." At least I hoped he didn't.

"Is Derek the young man with the beard that I've seen at Eric's a couple of times?"

I took a sip of my coffee. "He is."

"He's quite good-looking," Rebecca said. "He has lovely dark eyes."

I choked on my coffee. "Rebecca!" I sputtered.

"I can see," she said. She gave Everett a loving look across the table and then turned her attention to me. "I'm married," she added matter-of-factly, "not dead, my dear." She took the chair opposite me then and folded her hands primly in her lap. "I also heard what happened at the hotel. I'm sorry you had to find Mr. Lewis."

"Thank you," I said.

"Marcus is on the case," Everett said. He didn't frame the words as a question, which told me he already knew Marcus was investigating.

I nodded. "He is."

Rebecca reached over and patted my arm. "You said last night there was something you wanted to talk to us about. What is it?"

I gave my head a little shake to chase away the cobwebs. "Lewis Wallace, actually," I said. "Specifically, what can you tell me about the business he was considering opening here in town?"

"Not that much," Everett said, folding his newspaper and setting it beside him on the table. He was tall and lean with a close-cropped white beard and intense dark eyes. He reminded me of actor Sean Connery. "I haven't been very involved in the decision making for this particular project—mostly just a case of bad timing for me."

"I've been to all of the meetings," Rebecca added, "but I don't feel I know that much and that's the problem. I didn't like the fact that from my perspective, Mr. Wallace seemed to be stalling on providing more concrete details for his business—which suppliers would he be working with, what were his projected sales, what part of the country was he marketing to, did he have a distribution system in place? The basics really."

Once again I was impressed with Rebecca's business acumen. I shouldn't have been. Rebecca was very savvy about life and people in general and business in particular. She had been a hairdresser and she knew all about running a small business in a time when there hadn't been so many women doing it.

Everett nodded. "I had the same concerns as Rebecca. And I wanted to know more about Wallace's previous failed business. Why did it go under? What did he learn from the experience?" He set his coffee cup on the table. "Mind you, I'm not saying that that failure was necessarily a bad thing. Some people take a while to find the right fit for their skills."

"According to the Small Business Association, half of all businesses fail in the first five years," I said.

"That's right," he said. "That can be due to anything from not researching the market to not having a good business plan to not listening to customer feedback. I wanted to know if Mr. Wallace was aware of his weaknesses."

"Have we told you anything that helps?" Rebecca asked.

"I'm not sure," I admitted, tracing the rim of my coffee cup with one finger. "I'm trying to get a sense of what kind of businessman Lewis Wallace was. He's pretty much an enigma."

"You know that he was selling memorabilia? That was the business that failed."

I nodded. "I know there were some disgruntled customers and some accusations about the legitimacy of some of the things he was selling."

"It was more than that," Rebecca said. "There was a police investigation. And a couple of people sued."

"What happened?" I hadn't found any of this information in my cursory research online.

"The investigation didn't lead to any charges and the lawsuits were settled out of court, very recently as a matter of fact."

"That doesn't mean people still weren't angry," I said. Some people can hold a grudge for a long time.

"You're wondering if Mr. Wallace died because of a business deal gone wrong." Rebecca got up off her chair and got the coffeepot. She topped up her husband's cup and gestured at mine.

"Please," I said. I added more cream and sugar to my cup then leaned back in my seat, hands wrapped around the mug. I was stalling to come up with a diplomatic answer to Rebecca's question. "From my limited experience with the man and from what I've read about him, he seemed to be the kind of person to whom people reacted strongly."

"In other words, he could be a jerk," she said flatly.

I sighed. "Yes."

"How is the investigation going into Mr. Wallace's death? Has Marcus learned anything?"

"I'm not giving away any secrets by saying it's going very slowly," I said, once again choosing my words with care.

"Well I'm sure things are a bit more challenging because the medical examiner didn't immediately rule the death a homicide."

"Umm, how did you know that?" I asked.

Rebecca gave me what I thought of as her sweet-little-old-lady smile. "I have my sources."

Her source was likely Mary's daughter, Bridget, who was the publisher of the town paper. I had no idea who Bridget's source was. Neither did Marcus, which caused him a fair amount of frustration.

"Lewis Wallace's death could have been an accident." I tapped the side of my cup with one finger. "It's a bad idea to jump to conclusions."

"But it wasn't an accident," Everett said.

"There are a lot of unanswered questions," Rebecca added. "I think it a good thing that someone is looking for answers." She smiled again.

I smiled back at her. "Thank you both for answering them. And thank you for the coffee." I looked at Hercules. "Okay, Fuzzy Face. Let's go."

He made a face and gave an indignant meow.

"If you walk home by yourself you'll end up with wet feet," I reminded him.

He immediately looked at Rebecca.

"Oh, that's not a problem," she said. "I'll bring Hercules home later in the wagon."

"I'm sorry, the wagon? What wagon?" I had somehow lost the thread of the conversation.

"Oh my goodness, did I not show it to you?"

"No," I said, shaking my head.

"I can't believe I forgot," Rebecca said. "Maggie found me an old wooden Radio Flyer wagon at a flea market about a month ago. She cleaned it up and painted it for me. Red, of course. I'm going to use it to move my plants when I'm working in my garden. I can bring Hercules home in it. There isn't that much snow left in the backyard." She held up both hands as though everything was settled.

"I can't let you do that."

Everett raised an eyebrow. "Bad idea," he said softly.

Rebecca was studying me through narrowed eyes. "I don't understand," she said. "You *can't let* me?" Equal emphasis on the "can't" and the "let" in the sentence. "Kathleen, are you trying to say you don't trust me to bring Hercules home safely?"

"No," I said, feeling my face redden. I hadn't meant to offend her.

"You don't think I'm too feeble to pull a wagon with a little cat in it across the yard, then, do you?"

Crap on toast! I had offended Rebecca.

"No, no . . . I just . . . There's snow out there."

She gave a snort. "There's barely a dusting. I don't see a problem." She waited, head cocked to one side.

I wasn't quite sure what to say. I took a deep breath and slowly let it out. "I appreciate your offer to make sure Hercules gets home," I said carefully. "Thank you."

Rebecca smiled. "You're very welcome." She reached over and set a piece of bacon in front of Hercules. "I almost forgot. I have a pie for you," she said. "I'll go get it. It's in the pantry."

The cat gave me a smug look that told me he knew who'd won and bent his head over his bacon. Rebecca went to get the pie. I looked at Everett. "I was played, wasn't I?"

"Like a ninety-nine-cent kazoo," he said with a smile.

As I headed home through the backyard I saw Owen waiting for me on the railing of the back stoop. He had come out with me when I'd headed over to see Rebecca and Everett. He liked to do a morning survey of the yard. I had no idea what he was looking for but it was part of his daily routine. His nose twitched at the pie.

"It's people food," I told him as I unlocked the porch door.

He made a sound like a sigh.

I kicked off my shoes, hung up my jacket and set the pie on the counter, covering it with a clean dishtowel for the moment. I got another cup of coffee and decided it was probably a bit too early for pie. It was blueberry. I'd checked.

I took a seat at the table. "Based on what Rebecca told me, Lewis Wallace definitely made some enemies with his last business. Maybe one of them tracked him down here," I said. "Two people sued him and he was investigated by the police. He had to have left some unhappy customers in his wake."

Owen seemed to be more interested in working out a stubborn knot in the fur on his tail than hearing about what I'd learned. "I just feel if I knew a little more about the man I could maybe figure out whether his death was personal or business."

I tried to think of some way other than haunting the Internet to find more about Lewis Wallace the man. I couldn't come up with anything. I looked up from my coffee to find Owen sitting in the wooden basket from Burtis Chapman that had been filled with potatoes from his root cellar. I'd left the basket under the coat hooks to remind me to return it. "Owen, get out of there," I said.

The cat didn't budge an inch. He just continued to sit in the basket and wash his face. I set my cup down, went over and scooped him out. "Burtis puts food in that basket," I scolded. "You can't sit in it. We already had this conversation."

Owen squirmed to get down. I set him on the floor. He headed for the living room, where I knew he'd likely climb on the footstool—another place he wasn't supposed to sit. I went back to my coffee.

I thought about Burtis, who had showed up a couple of days before Ethan and the guys had arrived with the basket filled with potatoes that had spent the winter cool and dry in his root cellar. He'd stood in the porch and he had seemed to fill the space. "I hear you're going to have some extra mouths to feed," he'd said.

A basket of potatoes might have seemed like an odd gift, but not to me. Russet potatoes from Burtis Chapman's huge garden had a wonderful flavor and made delicious fries and hash browns. I would also have happily eaten them in a big bowl mashed with butter and a little salt and pepper.

Burtis Chapman was an intensely loyal man to his friends—including Marcus's father, Elliot Gordon, whom he'd known since they were boys. But he'd worked for Idris Blackthorne—Ruby's grandfather—as a young man. Idris had been the area bootlegger, among other things, and he'd had a reputation for coming down hard and fast on anyone who crossed him. There were some people in town who saw Burtis the same way.

I knew Burtis was a big football fan, a Vikings fan in particular, knowledgeable about stats and trades and who was injured in any given week. I wasn't sure if he followed college football or the Canadian league, but if he didn't there was at least a chance he'd know someone who did.

I looked in the direction of the living room. Was that why Owen had climbed into the potato basket? Was it his way of making me think of Burtis? I shook my head. No. That was a bit too much of a stretch. I was seeing connections where there weren't any, I told myself. Still, I couldn't quite shake the feeling that maybe I was right.

I did a load of laundry, cleaned the bathroom and dusted every-where. Ethan got up, muttered a good morning and foraged in the kitchen for breakfast—wearing a T-shirt for a change. After he'd eaten—two scrambled eggs with mushrooms and tomatoes, two cups of coffee and a slice of Rebecca's pie—he'd wandered into the living room to ask if he could do some laundry later.

"I kinda need some clean clothes to take with me," he said, scratching his stubbled chin.

"Go ahead," I said. "What time are you leaving?" The Flaming Gerbils were playing three shows in Milwaukee, about a four-and-a-half-hour drive away. They'd be back on Monday.

Ethan yawned and scratched one armpit. "I told the guys I'd pick them up at one o'clock." He looked around the room. "You want me to vacuum for you?" he asked.

"Seriously?" I said.

He shrugged. "Yeah. I figure it's the least I can do since I'm staying here and eating your food."

I grinned at him. "You're right. So yes and thank you."

I left for the library a bit more than an hour later. I gave Ethan a hug. "Have fun."

"Aren't you going to tell me to stay out of trouble?" he teased.

"You're a grown man now, not a little kid," I said. "I'm going to try harder to treat you that way."

"Plus, you know you're wasting time." His dark eyes gleamed.

I gave him a kiss on the cheek. "By the way, Rebecca will probably bring Hercules back in a little while."

He frowned. "How is she going to do that? The furball doesn't let anyone but you pick him up."

I smiled, getting a mental image of Rebecca pulling Hercules in her wagon. "I'm just going to let you see that for yourself," I said.

I stopped in at Eric's for coffee before I went to the library. Standing at the counter, I realized I had forgotten to bring my lunch or to even make it, for that matter. "Is it too late for a breakfast sandwich?" I asked Claire.

"I'm not sure," she said. "Hang on. Let me check with Eric."

Claire poked her head in the kitchen and was back in less than a minute. She smiled. "He says it will only be a few minutes."

I thanked her and dropped onto a stool to wait. The door to the café opened and Simon Janes walked in.

"Hi, Kathleen," he said. "This is a nice surprise, seeing you twice in less than a day."

"I talked to Mia last night," I said, swinging around on the stool so I was facing him.

He made a face. "Did she happen to tell you that she's met a guy?"

I laughed. "Yes, she did. She has a good head on her shoulders, thanks to you. Don't worry."

Simon pointed a finger at me. "That may be so, but any

questions about boys and anything related to them are going to be referred to you."

After Simon's father's death I'd moved into a surrogate-mother role with Mia, and I treasured our connection. I smiled. "That's fine with me."

Simon gave Claire his take-out order and then turned to me again. "I didn't tell you last night. I heard what happened at the hotel. You found Lewis Wallace's body."

I nodded. "I did."

"I'm sorry you had to go through that," he said. "Has Marcus figured out what happened yet?"

"He's still investigating."

"If you think it might help, I can ask around, see if I can find out anything else about the man." He picked up a sugar packet and flipped it over his fingers.

I didn't see the point in denying that I was interested in Lewis Wallace. But I didn't want to lead Simon on, either.

As if he could read my mind, Simon held up his hands and said, "As friends, Kathleen. No catch."

I didn't have a lot of other options at the moment. I nodded. "Thank you."

Claire came back with my food. I slid off the stool.

"I'll be in touch if I find out anything," Simon said.

I thanked him again and headed for the library, hoping I wasn't going to regret this.

chapter 10

Simon came into the library midmorning on Saturday. By that time I had already put out the new magazines, updated the anti-virus software on our computers and helped a mom-to-be find several books on baby care.

I knew from the expression on Simon's face that he'd found something. "That was fast," I said.

He smiled. "More good luck than good timing," he said. "I'm not even sure if what I learned is going to be of any use to you."

"What did you find out?" I asked. I'd learned so little about Lewis Wallace so far that anything Simon could tell me would help.

"Wallace's other business failed because basically he didn't pay any attention to it. When you start a business you need to be boots on the ground all the time. You need to be there, putting in the time, putting in the effort. He wasn't. They were really just using his name and image."

"That doesn't make him sound like a very good businessman."

Simon shook his head. "No, it doesn't. I think at the time he was just trying to exploit what little name recognition he had."

"So that might explain why the development committee was willing to consider making a deal with him even though he didn't have the best track record."

"It might."

"There's something else, isn't there?" I said. There was something in his tone. Skepticism, maybe? It was almost as if he knew something but wasn't sure whether or not he believed it.

"Two things, actually," he said. "I don't know if you knew, but there were a couple of lawsuits filed against Wallace's memorabilia business."

I nodded. "I knew."

"You know how long those things can take to move through the legal system." Simon patted his jacket pocket with one hand and I wondered if that's where his phone was.

"Years," I said. "But I thought those lawsuits had been settled out of court."

"They were. Just a few weeks ago, *by Lewis Wallace*."

It took me a moment to catch what he was getting at. "You mean by Wallace personally. Not by his insurance company."

Simon nodded.

I frowned at him. "But why now? And why did he use his own money? Was he just trying to cut his losses?"

"According to my source, it looked like the insurance company—and by extension Wallace—was probably going to win both cases. As for why now and why he used his own money, I have no idea."

"Maybe he had an attack of conscience." That didn't quite jibe with kicking a service dog in a bar, but it was all that I could come up with.

"Maybe," Simon said. His expression told me he didn't think it was likely.

"Wait a minute," I said, holding up a finger. "Where did he get the money?"

"That's the second thing. I found out how Wallace really made his money. I don't think he got rich playing football in Canada. He and some other investors made their real money investing in new businesses and ones that were looking to expand."

"So Wallace and his friends were angel investors?"

"Not exactly." Simon straightened the scarf at his neck. "First of all, an angel investor generally offers a lot more favorable loan terms than a bank or some other lender because most of the time the investment is in the person—the entrepreneur—not the actual business. Wallace and his group weren't doing that."

I didn't like what I was hearing.

"Angel investors are interested more in helping start-ups take their first steps and in seeing established businesses expand than they are in just maximizing profit."

That decidedly didn't fit with what I knew about Lewis Wallace.

Simon smiled. "You probably know where the term 'angel' comes from."

"Yes, I do know that," I said. I had been twisting my watch around my arm. I made myself stop and put one hand behind my back. "From the theater. From Broadway, to be specific. Angels invest in productions to help them reach the stage. I can think of a play my mother was part of that wouldn't have been staged without an angel." I also knew who had used her persuasive skills to convince that angel to bless the production.

"But you're saying Wallace wasn't lending money at a better rate than the banks."

"As far as I know he was charging *more* because the people who were borrowing from him had already been turned down by those kinds of conventional lenders or they knew they would be."

"It seems so . . . manipulative," I said.

"The way Wallace was doing business, it was. His loans all included a way to call in the loan on short notice."

"And if the business owner couldn't pay?"

"Then Wallace and his investor friends looted the company of everything that was worth anything. They'd make their money back and then some, plus for months before that they were getting above market rate interest."

"So there would be no company left," I said slowly. "No products or services to sell. No jobs for anyone."

"Businesses that had been in operation for decades, that had just hit a small financial bump, were essentially looted." Simon's expression was grim. "And it happens more than you think." He pulled a folded sheet of paper out of the pocket of his hoodie and handed it to me without comment.

It was a list of businesses. I recognized some names, several others I'd never heard of and one name I knew well. I looked up at Simon. "Redmond Signs was in Red Wing. They went under a little more than a year ago." I'd heard the name just recently, too, but I couldn't place where or when.

"More like they were held under," he said. He tapped the company name on the page with one finger. "I remember that one. The company had been in business for more than sixty years. They got a bit overextended buying some new equipment to print removable decals. Wallace and his partners swept in and in less than six months the company was gone."

"Red Wing isn't that far from here," I said as I folded the paper in half again.

"No, it isn't," Simon agreed. "A lot of people would have heard that Lewis Wallace might be doing business here."

I nodded, wondering how I was going to use what Simon had discovered.

His eyes narrowed. "Will this help?"

"It gives me somewhere to look, so yes."

He smiled. "My work here is done, then."

"It was good work," I said. "Thank you."

"Anytime, Kathleen," he said. "Remember that."

When I got home that afternoon after stopping for groceries I found Hercules on the bench in the porch, chin resting on the windowsill, looking morose. I set my two grocery bags on the floor and leaned down to stroke his fur. "It is kind of quiet without Ethan here drumming on pretty much everything and singing ninety percent of the time," I said.

Hercules murped his agreement.

I tried not to think about how quiet it was going to be when my baby brother went home.

It was a cold and windy day and neither the cat nor I felt inclined to go back outside, so we ended up at the table with my laptop. Me with a hot chocolate piled high with The Jam Lady's marshmallow and Hercules with a couple of sardine crackers. "You're a pretty good research partner," I said as I gave him a scratch under his chin.

"Mrr," he replied. It seemed he already knew that.

Since the company had gone under, there was no website for Redmond Signs anymore, but a little digging did produce a newspaper article on the demise of the company. When I saw the accompanying photographs, I knew why the name Redmond had twigged for me. In one of them, part of a timeline of the company's history, there was a gawky teenager, skinny, all but hiding behind his grandfather, who had begun Redmond Signs when he wasn't much older than the kid who was all arms and legs. The older man was tall like his grandson with dark skin, graying hair and the barrel-chested build that suggested maybe he had played football.

I raised an inquiring eyebrow at Hercules. "Do you think Redmond Senior was a football player at some time? Could that have had anything to do with Lewis Wallace's investment in the company?"

He wrinkled his whiskers at me. He didn't seem convinced.

I might have passed right by the older man's grandson. In the caption for the photo he was identified as Michael. I probably would have if the photo hadn't been in color. It was the teen's eyes that caught my attention. They were a vivid blue. That's when I realized why the name Redmond was familiar. I'd met Michael Redmond, except he was going by the name Zach. He was Maggie's friend, the bartender at The Brick.

I leaned against the back of my chair and stretched one arm over my head. It could have been a coincidence that Lewis Wallace had ended up at a bar where Zach/Michael worked. On the other hand . . .

"I need to talk to him," I said to Hercules.

The cat's response was to stretch out a paw and bat my cell phone closer, then he jumped down and headed back to the porch. Clearly the next part of this fact-finding mission was up to me.

I picked up the phone and called Maggie. "Hi," she said. "I was just talking about you. Well, actually, about Owen and Hercules. Another customer came in and asked about the calendar. I really think Ruby is going to have to do a second one."

Owen and Hercules had posed for a series of photos taken by my friend, artist Ruby Blackthorne, at various landmarks around Mayville Heights—the library, of course, the Stratton Theatre, on the walking trail along the river—with the resulting photos made into a calendar to promote the town. Everett Henderson had funded the project. The response had been even better than we'd hoped. The first printing had sold out and so had the second. And people were still asking for copies or wondering if there was going to be a version for next year.

"I guess that will depend on whether or not Ruby and Everett can reach a deal with the 'talent.'" I laughed. "Sometimes I feel like I'm just part of the celebrity entourage."

"Only you carry sardine crackers instead of a water bottle," Maggie teased. "What's up?"

"I need to go back to The Brick. Do you have plans tonight?" I picked up my hot chocolate and realized the mug was empty.

"Nothing I can't change," she said. "Does this mean you've decided to buy yourself some peacock feathers?"

"No, it does not," I said firmly. I explained about Zach Redmond and his connection to Lewis Wallace. "I know he's a friend, Mags, and I'm not saying he killed Wallace, it's just an awfully big coincidence."

"You're right." I heard her exhale on the other end of the phone. "You should talk to Zach, and I do want to come with you."

"Thanks," I said. It would be a lot easier having her with me. Not only did Maggie know Zach, but she was funny and kind and wherever she went she just drew people to her. Which probably explained Ethan's attraction, now that I thought about it.

"What about Roma?" Maggie said. "The three of us haven't been on a road trip in ages."

"That's a good idea," I said. "I'll call her and get back to you."

I ended the call and made one to Roma.

"How do you feel about a road trip?" I asked.

"Yes," she said almost before I finished asking the question.

"You don't even know where we're going."

"I don't care." She sounded a little frazzled. "Just tell me what time and I'll pick up you and Maggie."

I pulled my legs up underneath me and shifted sideways on the chair. "What's going on?"

"My living room has been invaded by ginormous hockey players who can somehow fly down the ice at lightning speed and swat a little piece of frozen rubber into a net but can't walk across the floor without bumping into something."

I stifled the impulse to laugh, remembering that Marcus had mentioned three of Eddie's former teammates were in town. Roma and I settled on a time and I took her up on her offer to pick Maggie and me up in her SUV. Unlike my truck, it had heated seats. I sent Maggie a text letting her know Roma would be stopping for her and when. Then I got up to make another cup of hot chocolate.

I heard a noise behind me and turned to see Owen at the basement door. He cocked his head and seemed surprised to see me.

"I live here, too, remember?" I said.

He wandered over to his bowl, peered into it and then nudged it with a paw before looking at me again.

"It's not supper time," I said.

The microwave buzzed and I took my mug out. Owen crossed the floor and sat at my feet. He meowed loudly, then looked at the cupboard where I kept the stinky crackers.

"Two," I said, holding up the corresponding number of

fingers. "And I'm only giving you those because your brother already had two."

I got out the two kitty treats and set them on the floor in front of me. He gave a small murp of thanks and then bent his head to sniff each cracker. He'd been that way since he was a kitten, always suspicious, it seemed, that his food might be off somehow.

" 'There is nothing either good or bad, but thinking makes it so,' " I said.

A furry gray ear twitched, but that was the only reaction I got. It seemed Owen wasn't a fan of Shakespeare.

After I finished my drink and gave Owen a scratch behind the ears *and* carried him upstairs because he was suddenly too tired to walk, I called Marcus. "I have to cancel our plans for tonight."

"Is everything okay?" he asked.

"I'm going out to The Brick to talk to the bartender. He has a connection to Lewis Wallace. Don't worry, Roma and Maggie are going with me."

Marcus paused for a long moment. "Zach Redmond," he said at last. "He was working the night we were all there."

"Yes," I said.

"I already talked to him. There's nothing there, Kathleen."

"I still want to talk to him myself."

"Okay," he said after another silence. "Just come up when you're done. It doesn't matter how late it is."

Roma pulled into the driveway at five to nine. I climbed into the backseat of her SUV. Maggie turned and smiled at me.

"Thank you for coming with me, both of you," I said.

"Anytime," Roma said as she backed out onto the street. She was wearing a heavy off-white sweater with a quilted purple vest. Her dark hair was cut in a sleek bob.

"Do you remember the first time we did something like this?" Maggie asked.

"You mean the time you and Kathleen hijacked me," Roma retorted, brown eyes fixed on the road. I could see a smile pulling at the corners of her mouth. We'd had a version of this conversation before.

Maggie and I had been following someone—at least we were trying to—but her car wouldn't start and it was before I had my truck. Maggie had dragged me over to Roma's SUV and convinced her to give chase.

Maggie laughed. "You don't have a leg to stand on when it comes to questioning our adventures because the one with Faux Eddie brought you and the real Eddie together."

Maggie had crafted a full-sized replica of Eddie for a display at the town's Winterfest celebration. Getting the not-real Eddie from Maggie's studio all the way downtown had started a rumor that Roma and the hockey player were "seeing" each other. Eventually it wasn't a rumor anymore.

The smile Roma had been trying to stifle got loose. She was always that way when Eddie's name was mentioned.

Roma managed to find a parking space squeezed in between two extended-cab pickups in the crowded parking lot. "I want fries," she announced the moment we stepped inside The Brick. Once again it was crowded and loud.

We made our way over to the bar. Somehow there were two free stools and a guy with beautiful gray eyes and a sleeve of tattoos up his left arm slid off his seat next to the empty two and gave it to Maggie. She smiled at him and he almost fell over a chair as he walked away with his friends.

"How do you do that?" I said.

She looked at me genuinely confused. "Do what?"

"Turn men into goofy ten-year-olds," Roma said.

"I don't do that," Maggie said.

"Yes, you do," Roma retorted as she slid onto a vacant stool. "It's your superpower."

Zach came down the bar and it was his turn to smile when he caught sight of Maggie. "Hi, Maggie," he said. "What can I get you?"

She pointed from herself to me to Roma. "White wine, white wine, ginger ale and a large fries."

"No problem," he said.

While Zach and Maggie made small talk I studied the bartender. As I'd noticed the first time I'd seen him, his deep blue eyes were his most striking feature.

SOFIE KELLY

The band started to play as Zach slid a glass of white wine in front of me. They weren't as good as The Flaming Gerbils but they weren't bad. The number of customers looking for a drink was already thinning out as people started listening to the music.

"You're Kathleen, right?" he said. "You were here last Friday night. I never forget a face." He snapped his fingers. "Your brother and his band sat in with Backroads last weekend. The Hamsters?"

"The Flaming Gerbils," I said.

He grinned. "Now, how could I forget that?"

A waitress came from the kitchen then and handed him a basket of fries. He set it in front of me with a flourish since I was sandwiched between Maggie and Roma. Roma immediately grabbed a couple of the French fries, dipping them in the little metal bowl of spicy ketchup.

"I owe you an apology," I said, taking a sip of my wine.

"Why? What did you do?" he asked. He was flirting with me, leaning in, smiling a lot.

"Not me," I said. "But one of my friends was the guy who punched that guy who kicked the service dog."

"Then you don't owe me an apology, but I do owe your friend a beer on the house next time he's in here. The guy was a jerk."

"That sounds like you knew him," Maggie said.

"I know his type," Zach said. "Big shot ex-jock thought the rules didn't apply to him."

"You know he's dead now?"

"You know what they say about karma," he said, shrugging one shoulder. He gave me another smile. "If I can get you anything else, let me know." He moved down the bar and once he was out of earshot Maggie leaned close to my ear.

"Did you get what you needed?" she asked.

I thought about the gleam in Zach Redmond's eye when he'd said, *"You know what they say about karma."* "It's a start," I said.

chapter 11

Zach stayed busy after that. It wasn't difficult to see he was avoiding Maggie and maybe me as well. "I'm sorry," I said to Maggie. "I know you like Zach but I have a feeling there's something he didn't tell us. His disdain for Lewis Wallace is too deep to be just over him kicking that service dog." I had told them about Redmond Signs on the drive out to the bar.

Maggie ran a finger down the side of her glass. "I know," she said. "You think it has something to do with his grandfather's business. But I just can't see Zach killing someone. He helps out with the seniors' yoga class. I know he's a bit of a flirt, but he's not a creep."

"Lewis Wallace died from an allergic reaction, didn't he?" Roma asked.

"Yes," I said, snagging three fries from the basket. Roma had already eaten half of them.

"So maybe Zach didn't kill the man. Not deliberately, I mean. Maybe when Wallace couldn't breathe Zach didn't realize the significance and just walked away. Maybe it was a crime of omission, not a crime of commission."

I shrugged but didn't say anything. Smashing food into someone's face was a deliberate act. So was keeping an EpiPen away from someone who needed it.

Roma's words seemed to cheer Maggie up a little. "When are the guys coming back?" she asked.

"Sometime on Monday," I said.

"Aside from the thing with Wallace and the dog it was fun Friday night. We should do it again before Ethan leaves." She looked at Roma. "At a time when you and Eddie can be there."

Roma nodded. "I'd like that."

"We could even go to Barry's Hat," Maggie said, nudging me with her elbow.

"I like that idea," I said, making a face at her. "And Ethan wanted to check the place out."

"Oh, he already did. That's where we went the night we were celebrating Derek being cleared as a suspect."

We?

"I didn't know you went out with the guys that night."

She reached over and grabbed a French fry. "Yeah," she said. "Ethan invited me and it sounded like fun." She smiled. "It was."

So Maggie had gone out with Ethan and the guys. Maybe Ethan's interest in Maggie had gotten a bit of inadvertent encouragement.

On my other side, Roma was still eating the crispy fries as though she expected them to disappear without warning.

"Roma, did you eat anything today?" I asked.

"Yes," she said. Then she frowned. "Maybe. I'm not sure. I know I cooked a lot. Hockey players eat a lot. Even ex–hockey players."

I pushed the basket sideways so it was directly in front of her. I had a feeling Roma had done a lot of cooking and very little eating for the past several hours. "Maybe they could all go to Fern's for breakfast tomorrow. The big breakfast sounds like just the thing for them."

Roma licked ketchup off of her thumb. "Maybe I should go to Fern's for breakfast. A big breakfast sounds like just the thing for *me*."

Maggie and Roma dropped me off at Marcus's house at about ten thirty. I hugged them both and thanked them for their help and I promised I would talk to Ethan and work out a way for us all to get together before he went home.

As I climbed out of the SUV, Maggie turned and said, "You know, I still have those strands of fairy lights from Roma and Eddie's wedding."

"And, as you know, my living room is the perfect spot for a wedding," Roma added.

"What are you two, the marriage police?" I asked.

"Yes," they both said and then dissolved in laughter.

Maggie and Roma had conspired to get Marcus and me to a happily ever after from pretty much the moment he and I had met. Roma had paired us up to volunteer with the feral cats at Wisteria Hill and Maggie had sent Marcus and me on our first date of sorts by giving Marcus her ticket to the final concert at the Wild Rose Summer Music Festival but "forgetting" to tell me what she'd done. They had all but wrapped me up with a red ribbon and deposited me on his doorstep, and the only reason *that* hadn't happened was because the idea hadn't occurred to them.

"Good night," I said as I closed the car door. I waved over my shoulder as I walked up the driveway. I was pretty sure they were still laughing as they drove away.

Micah was waiting for me on the railing of the back deck, her eyes gleaming in the darkness. "Hi, puss," I said.

She meowed a hello and I stroked her marmalade-colored fur. Once again I felt a twist of guilt knot in my chest. I'd suspected very early that the little cat had the same sort of abilities as my two did and I wasn't really that surprised when she had winked out of sight one day. But I hadn't said a word to Marcus. I kept avoiding it, making excuses, and I didn't really have a good reason. I trusted him, didn't I?

Micah jumped down from her perch and crossed the deck to the back door. She looked over her shoulder at me and meowed once again. I knew she was telling me to hurry up.

Marcus smiled when I stepped into the kitchen and pulled me into a hug. "Hi," he said. "I didn't think you'd be this early."

"Roma ate all the French fries so we figured it was time to leave," I said.

"Want some hot chocolate or are you too full of fries?" he asked as I shrugged off my jacket and draped it over the back of a chair. Micah had disappeared somewhere. I hoped not literally.

"First of all, there is no such thing as being too full for hot chocolate," I told him. "And second, Roma really did eat most of the fries. It seems that she's been feeding some of Eddie's former teammates but hasn't been feeding herself."

He nodded as he moved to the refrigerator for the milk. "The guys I told you about. They came for a quick trip to take a look at the curriculum Eddie's been working on for his hockey school."

Eddie, nicknamed Crazy Eddie Sweeney in his playing days, had been working on an idea for a year-round hockey development school for a long time, but now that he had Everett Henderson involved it seemed a lot closer to reality.

"I hope the school works out for him," I said.

"I think it will," Marcus said as he reached for a mug. He poured the milk and stuck the cup in the microwave. Then he turned around. "Are you going to tell me what you found out?"

"I didn't find out anything concrete." Micah came in from the hall with what looked like a small scrap of paper stuck to one ear. She came back to the table, I patted my lap and she jumped up. I took the bit of paper off her ear and she shook her head vigorously.

"First of all, how would Zach Redmond have even known where Lewis Wallace was staying?" Marcus asked. "And if he *had* somehow gotten the information, how could he have known that Wallace was wandering around because he couldn't sleep?"

"He could have made an educated guess about the hotel," I said. "It is the nicest one in town. Maybe he just went there to talk to the man. The rest could have been a crime of opportunity."

"In other words, you still think he could be involved?"

I nodded. "I do." I explained Zach's comment about karma. Before Marcus could say anything I held up the hand that wasn't stroking Micah's fur. "Yes, I know that's about as substantial as dandelion fluff."

He put a heaping spoonful of hot chocolate mix into the cup of hot milk and stirred. "I'm not sure that proves anything, Kathleen. Lots of people feel strongly about animals being mistreated, especially service animals. Rebecca, for example. Roma. Derek. *You.*"

"Rebecca is one of the most kindhearted people I know.

184

She puts together shelters for the feral cats. She's on the board of directors of the animal rescue. As far as Roma goes, she's a vet. She was taking care of the cats out at Wisteria Hill long before she bought the place from Everett. Derek's dad is a veteran and most important he was sorry about what happened. Zach isn't even sorry that Wallace is dead."

Marcus set the cup in front of me. He leaned down to kiss me. "Point taken," he said.

Micah made an annoyed sound and jumped down to the floor again.

"No more talking about the case for tonight," I said. I knew there wasn't anything else I could do at the moment and going over what little I did have wasn't getting me anywhere.

"Deal," Marcus said, sitting down in the chair next to me. "Tell me about the rest of your day."

I took a sip of the hot chocolate. It was good: dark chocolate, not too sweet and there were two fat marshmallows on top. "Let me see. We discovered licorice in the book drop, and before you ask, I don't have a clue why. It took fourteen e-mails but Patricia and I have settled on what cookies will be served at the opening of the quilt festival. There's a large truck tire in the middle of the gazebo. And somebody returned a book on minimalism with a list of all the things on their Amazon wish list stuck inside as a bookmark."

"What kind of licorice?"

"What kind of licorice? I gave you irony, a mystery and cookies and you want to know what kind of licorice?"

He shrugged. "I like licorice."

We talked about our respective days for a few minutes until I finished my hot chocolate. Marcus put my empty mug in the sink and pulled me to my feet. "Do you want a shower or a bath?"

"Bath," I said at once. I loved his big, deep, claw-footed bathtub.

Over his shoulder Micah looked at me, seemed to shimmer for a moment and then disappeared.

"Go run the water, then," he said. "I'll lock up out here." He looked around for the cat. "Where did she go?"

"Maybe she's in the living room," I said. Was my face getting red?

The moment he was out of the room the little ginger tabby reappeared. I knew what the cat was trying to tell me.

"She's right here hiding under the table," I called.

Marcus came back into the room shaking his head. "I can't believe I looked right past her. Maybe I need glasses."

The cat continued to watch me and I felt that knot of guilt again. *As soon as this case is settled,* I told myself. I had a feeling all three cats were going to hold me to that.

🐾

Marcus made breakfast the next morning—pancakes with applesauce, thick-cut bacon and lots of coffee. I sat at the table in the sweatshirt and jeans I kept at his place and thought how easily I could get used to mornings like this.

Before he drove me home, Marcus handed me my own take-out coffee cup filled with coffee. "You're spoiling me," I said.

He nodded. "All part of my plan."

After he dropped me off he was going to stop at the station for a minute. I didn't ask why. We agreed he'd be back after lunch and we'd go to the market.

⁂

Even though there was still snow on the ground and a cold crispness to the air, the market was busy. "I need to talk to Thorsten," Marcus said.

"Go ahead," I said. "I'm going to walk around for a bit. I'll find you later." I headed over to the Sweet Things kiosk. I'd had a couple of texts from Ethan letting me know things were going well. Maybe some celebratory cupcakes would be a good thing, I decided. And a good excuse to talk to Georgia.

"Hi, Kathleen," she said. "What can I tempt you with?"

"I was thinking a half-dozen double chocolate," I said, "but now that I'm here how about four of those, four mocha fudge and four lemon."

"Excellent choices." She began to box up the cupcakes. "I hope I didn't get your brother in trouble over those muffins he bought," she said, ducking her head.

"You didn't."

She gave me a sideways glance. "I think he has a bit of a crush on Maggie."

I laughed. "I think you're right."

Georgia's expression turned serious. "This will probably sound odd, but I'm kind of glad I had that . . . encounter with Lewis Wallace at Fern's."

It was the last thing I would have expected to hear. Wallace had harassed her all the way from the parking lot and acted offended that she wasn't interested in his advances.

"Why?" I said. Georgia set the first box of cupcakes on the counter and reached for another container.

She shrugged. "I don't know if this will make sense, but after everything that happened with my in-laws I've been looking over my shoulder for what feels like years wondering if I'd be able to deal with them, with anyone coming after Emmy and me again. What I learned from that . . . that creep—I'm sorry, but it's the only word to describe him—is that I can take care of myself and Emmy and I have good friends if I need backup." Her cheeks were pink but she held her head high.

I leaned across the counter and gave her a hug. "Anytime you need backup just yell," I said. Out of the corner of my eye I saw Larry Taylor hovering around and it occurred to me that maybe Ethan wasn't the only person with a crush.

I paid Georgia, set the two boxes of cupcakes in my canvas shopping bag and resumed wandering around. I made my way around two teachers from the middle school in an animated discussion about onion sets and discovered Burtis Chapman and Lita Clarke, Everett's assistant, at the stall belonging to The Jam Lady. Lita was insisting that Burtis didn't need two jars of marmalade, and he was buying those and some plum jam as well in a show of stubbornness.

I touched Lita on the shoulder and she smiled. "Hello, Kathleen, how are you?" she said.

"I'm well," I said, "Thank you. Could I borrow Burtis for a minute?"

"Of course you can," she said. "In fact, I may let you keep the old coot."

Burtis just laughed. "You can't get by without me," he said.

Lita patted his cheek. "You just keep telling yourself that."

Burtis and I started to walk. "What do you need?" he asked. That was Burtis. He got straight to the point.

"What do you know about Canadian football?" I could have looked up the information, but this would be faster.

"This have anything to do with that Wallace fellow's death?" He was wearing his battered Vikings cap.

"Maybe."

His eyes narrowed. "What're you after?"

I shifted my shopping bag to my other hand, careful not to disturb the cupcakes. "Right now, just information."

"Fair enough. First of all, in Canadian football the field is larger—wider and longer. Second, the end zone is bigger."

"Is that it?" I asked.

Burtis shook his head. "Not even close. Up there you only get three downs to make ten yards. Not four."

"So Canadian football is more pass-oriented."

He gave me an approving smile. "You learn quick," he said.

He eyed me for a moment. "What kind of information are you really lookin' for?"

I wasn't exactly sure *what* I was looking for. Melanie had told me that Wallace had "supposedly made a bunch of money" playing in Canada, which didn't exactly jibe with the whole loaning-money-to-small-businesses scheme he'd been involved in. Simon had said he didn't think Wallace had gotten rich playing in the CFL. Marcus liked to say two of the most common reasons for murder were love and money. Was money the reason Lewis Wallace had been killed? I had no idea.

I stopped walking and turned to face Burtis. "I know Lewis Wallace wasn't good enough to play in the NFL, but was he good enough to be a star in Canada?"

Burtis took off his cap, smoothed down what little hair he had and put it back on again. "If you're asking if the man became some kind of superstar up there, I can promise you the answer is no. Football is not big business in Canada. Never has been."

"What do you mean?" I said.

"I mean your average player in the CFL makes less than a hundred thousand dollars a year. Woulda been a lot less in Wallace's day."

We started walking again, dodging my neighbor, Mike Justason, and his boys.

"So Lewis Wallace didn't make his money playing football."

Burtis shook his head. "No, girl, he didn't. Whatever money

the man had came after he stopped playing." He eyed me for a moment. "This help at all?"

"It might," I said. I smiled. "Thank you. I'll be out for another game of pinball soon."

He pointed at me. One of his huge hands was large enough to cover my head. "I'm not going to take it easy on you next time," he warned.

I wasn't fooled by his stern expression. Like Lita, I patted his cheek. "You just keep telling yourself that."

I could hear him laughing as I walked away.

Marcus made supper at my house and we played War, a card game Eddie's daughter, ten-year-old Sydney, had taught him. Marcus lost.

He slumped in his chair. "How did you do that?" he asked. "This is a game of chance, not a game a skill, and you still beat me." He was referring to the fact that I regularly beat him at road hockey and pinball and I'd beaten him at cup stacking at Roma and Eddie's wedding—another thing Syd had taught him.

Marcus narrowed his eyes at Owen and Hercules. "Are you helping her somehow?" Hercules got up from the spot by my chair where he'd been lying, flicked his tail and left the room. Owen yawned as though the question bored him.

"Did you win when you played Syd?" I asked.

"Not exactly." His gaze didn't quite meet mine.

"You either did or you didn't," I said as I gathered our mugs. "It's not really a sliding scale."

"Okay, I didn't."

I kissed him as I moved past him on the way to the sink. "Maybe you're just not lucky."

He caught my hand and pulled me onto his lap. "Maybe I just used up all my luck on more important things," he said before he kissed me.

Mary was working with me the next morning at the library. "What do you think about Zach Redmond?" I asked. I figured she probably knew him since she'd danced at the club more than once. We were sorting the books from the book drop. At least there hadn't been any licorice in it this time.

"You mean do I think he could have killed that a-hole your brother's friend punched?"

Trust Mary to get right to the point. I set the book I was holding down on the counter. "Since you put it that way, yes."

Mary shook her head. "He's a good kid and cute as a bug's ear but I don't think he has the ambition to actually carry out a crime. My mother would have said he's not too work-brittle."

"Which means?" I asked.

"He's too lazy to put in the effort it would take to kill someone."

The guys got back just after lunch. They came into the library, Milo in his cool-dude shades, Derek looking preoccupied and Ethan bouncing with energy like Tigger from the Winnie-the-Pooh books. It was easy to see things had gone well.

I gave Ethan a hug. "Did you miss me?" he asked.

I pretended to think about the question. "Let me see. No one's six"—I held up the corresponding number of fingers—"different hair products on the side of my tub. Which, by the way, is probably more than Milo travels with. No cupcake crumbs, muffin crumbs or cookie crumbs all over my kitchen floor and no one drinking all the coffee before I even get my first cup."

He held up a finger. "First of all, I do not leave cookie crumbs, muffin crumbs or I forgot what the first one was all over the floor." He paused for effect. "Owen always gets them before they hit the floor." He gave his head a shake. "And if you think this much pretty comes without upkeep, well, you are very, very mistaken."

I laughed, shaking my own head. "Yes, I missed you," I said.

He gave me a brief rundown of the three shows. Mary was at the front desk and by the time Ethan had finished telling me about their trip somehow she and Milo had gotten into a conversation about kickboxing. He turned to Ethan. "What was that thing you tried when we were in New York? It was some kind of martial art."

"It was hot yoga," Ethan said.

"I've been telling Maggie she should add a hot yoga class," Mary said. "I tried it the last time I was in Chicago."

Why didn't I know that? I wondered. And what was hot yoga?

Derek joined me. Ethan had been pulled into Milo's conversation with Mary.

"It sounds as though things went well," I said.

"Better than that," he said. "There was a record producer at one of the shows."

"Was he interested in the band?"

Derek shrugged. "Maybe. He didn't make any commitment but he's going to be in Boston next month and he's coming to hear us again."

There was something about the way he said "us" that caught my attention.

"Us?" I asked.

Derek nodded. "Milo and Ethan—and Devon—want me to join the band permanently."

"Did you say yes?"

Derek was very talented, there was no question about that, but he didn't have Jake's easy-going personality. *And whoever the guys hire to replace Jake is none of your business,* I reminded myself.

"I need to think about it," Derek said. "I have a lot of things on the go, other opportunities."

"I hope everything works out for you," I said.

Mary seemed to be sharing some kind of kicking technique

with Milo and Ethan. Or maybe it was a dance move. I decided I didn't want to know.

Ethan tried whatever movement it was that Mary had demonstrated and four books fell off the desk onto the floor.

I laughed. "I swear, one of these days he's going to fall off the stage when he's performing."

Derek grinned. "Who says he hasn't?" His smile faded as he studied me for a moment. "Kathleen, can I ask you a personal question?"

"I guess so," I said.

"How did you do it? I mean, being a teenager with two new siblings? Most kids would have resented the heck out of them, but you guys are so tight."

"Oh, I did resent the heck out of them," I said. "But they were so little and they'd stop crying for me before they'd stop for anyone else. I used to get up and watch those late, late cheesy horror movies on TV. The two of them were always awake. I'd take them into the living room with me. Which is probably why both Ethan and Sara are night owls now." I smiled at the memory. "They're my family. I'd do anything for family."

Something hardened in Derek's expression. He nodded. "I know. Me too."

chapter 12

Burtis showed up at the library right after lunch. He set a small metal box on the circulation desk. "Found something I thought you might be interested in," he said.

I recognized the box. We used similar ones to store the oldest newspapers in our collection. I lifted the lid. Inside I found three copies of *Phil Major's College Football Preview*. Each one was encased in a plastic sleeve, a piece of corrugated cardboard at its back and what I recognized as acid-free tissue separating the front and back covers from the rest of the pages.

I looked up at Burtis. "These magazines are in excellent condition."

"I got some older than you are," he said with a grin.

I carefully removed one from the box. "I don't recognize the magazine."

"Unless you're a big ball fan you wouldn't," he said. "They do a college football edition and one for the pros. Been puttin' them out since 1973. Phil Major wrote for *Sports Illustrated* in the sixties and then went to work for ABC Sports after that. He died about ten years ago. *Sports Illustrated* bought the magazine and kept the name. I have every issue right up to the most recent two. These three have articles with references to Lewis Wallace back in his college days. I thought they might save you some time."

I carefully removed one of the magazines from the box. The librarian in me was intrigued even without my desire to know more about Lewis Wallace. "Do you know where he played his college ball?" I asked.

Burtis nodded. "Saint Edwin University. It's in Pennsylvania. Good football school. Wallace got a degree in business. The boy was a decent player pretty much all four years he was there. Had a couple scouts lookin' at him in his freshman year but in the end he was just too small. He did stay and even got his degree but he struggled with the academics and had to be tutored to graduate."

He patted the side of the metal box. "There's a mention of a cheating incident Wallace was supposedly involved in during sophomore year." He smiled. "Don't mean to ruin the ending but it didn't amount to anything."

"Thank you, Burtis," I said. "I'll be very careful with your magazines and I'll get them back to you as soon as I can."

"I know you will," he said. "I hope you find something to help."

When I got home that evening, I discovered that Ethan was making spaghetti sauce, Derek was on his phone, Hercules was hiding under that table, Owen smelled like oregano and Milo was standing on a kitchen chair washing the ceiling above my stove.

Milo was the only one who didn't avoid my gaze. "Trust me, you really don't want to know," he said. Since I saw no need for bandages or the fire department, I decided he was right.

After supper Milo and Derek headed to their bed-and-breakfast, and Ethan decided to go for a walk. I'd taken Burtis's magazines upstairs to my bedroom. I set the storage container on the bed and pointed at the cats. "Stay on the floor," I said. "These belong to Burtis and I don't want anything to happen to them. That means no kitty paw prints, no kitty drool and no kitty hair anywhere near these magazines."

Hercules made disgruntled grumbles and retreated to the closet, probably to rearrange my shoes again. Owen made a show of washing his face even though he'd already done that downstairs. I could see him sneak peeks at me from time to time.

SOFIE KELLY

I was on my second article when Marcus called. He was going to be testifying in a case that went back more than two years and the prosecuting attorney was going over every tiny detail with him.

"We're taking a break," he said. "I just wanted to hear your voice."

"I'm glad you called," I said. "Burtis loaned me several magazines. I'm reading about Lewis Wallace."

"Have you discovered anything yet?"

I shook my head even though he couldn't see me. "Both articles I've read so far are pretty short. The most interesting thing was a photo of Lewis Wallace in his freshman year where he looks more like sixteen than nineteen." Wallace had been standing in front of a large brick building next to a large wall plaque with what I guessed was the college seal featuring the words "Virtus, Veritas, Honestas."

Marcus lowered his voice. "I've been looking into some of the people who lost their businesses to Wallace and his partners, but so far I haven't come across anyone I think might have murdered the man."

"If I find anything at all in the last magazine I'll let you know," I promised.

I'd just said good night to Marcus and laid my phone down on the bed when Owen launched himself from the floor. The metal storage box went over sideways and though I thought the top was secure, it opened and the third plastic-covered magazine slid onto the bed.

Owen made a wide circle around the box and the magazines and made his way up to the pillows.

"Hey! What did I say?" I asked. Burtis's magazine seemed to be fine.

"Merow," the cat replied.

"Exactly!" I retorted. I didn't have a clue what Owen's response had been but given the way he was ducking his head and looking everywhere but at me I was pretty sure he knew what he'd done was wrong.

I pointed at the door. "Out," I said, maybe a bit more dramatically than was needed.

Owen walked to the side of the bed, jumped down and left, complaining all the way. I got up and closed the door, peeking in the closet on the way by to see that Hercules was asleep, curled up on my favorite black pumps.

I picked up the magazine that had fallen out of the storage box and slipped it from the protective cover. It turned out to contain a short article about whether or not college athletes were getting meaningful degrees, or as the author of the piece asked, just a useless piece of paper so they managed to stay academically eligible to play. The article referenced the cheating scandal at Saint Edwin University during the previous football season. Lewis Wallace and two other members of the team had been accused of selling the answers to an accounting final—a required course for many of the players—to their team members, the same way they were alleged to have sold the answers to the midterm. As Burtis had already told me, Wallace turned out not to have been involved.

My phone rang then and I stretched to reach it. It was Melanie Davis.

"I'm sorry to bother you, Kathleen," she said, "but I have a potential quilt show problem."

"What is it?" I asked. I thought Patricia had gone over every detail. What could have gone wrong?

"Our chef tried the cookie recipes that Patricia dropped off. The lemon crinkle top ones are fine but he thinks the almond shortbread are too crumbly when the recipe is changed to make so many at once. And it's just not practical to make them in small batches. For what it's worth, I agree with him."

I put the magazine I'd been reading back in its protective sleeve. "How can I help?"

"Before I tell Patricia, I need a third opinion. I know she doesn't like last-minute changes and I'm hoping there's strength in numbers."

"I can come down and try a cookie right now if that helps."

"Are you sure you don't mind?" Melanie asked. I could hear voices in the background, which told me she was still at the St. James.

"You're offering me cookies," I said. "I don't mind."

I told her I'd be there in a few minutes and ended the call. I put all the issues of Burtis's magazines back in their storage container and made sure the lid was secure. I opened the closet door partway. Hercules in turn opened one eye and yawned.

"I have to go down to the hotel for a few minutes. I won't be long. Ethan will be back . . ." I had no idea when Ethan would be back. "At some point," I finished.

Hercules yawned again.

There was no sign of Owen in the hallway, the living room or the kitchen. He was probably in his lair in the basement, plotting something like the mustache-twirling villain in an old black-and-white movie. Or maybe he was chewing on a catnip chicken. I knew I was guilty of attributing human motivations to much of Hercules's and Owen's behaviors, when sometimes they were just being regular cats.

When I arrived at the St. James I checked at the front desk and the staff member working there told me that Melanie was in her office and I should head down. The lobby was busy with guests coming and going from their rooms and people heading to the restaurant and the lounge. I felt something brush against my leg, stepped to the left and almost bumped into two men pulling their suitcases, heads bent over their phones. I turned down the hall toward Melanie's office and the crush of people was gone, which meant there was only one explanation when once again I felt something brush against my leg.

I stopped and looked around. There was no sign of a certain devious furball, no indication that there was a cat in the hallway at all, but I knew he was there. Owen had stowed away in the truck. He was getting a lot better at it, I thought. In the past he would have given himself away, made a sound, knocked something over. I would have realized he was beside me on the seat, silent and invisible. He must have been in the kitchen when I left, walking out beside me.

"Owen, show yourself," I hissed. Of course he didn't.

I leaned forward and swept my arm all around in front of me a few inches above floor level, hoping I'd touch him even as I knew he was sitting just beyond my grasp, likely amused by my effort.

An older woman I took to be a visitor at the hotel came down the hallway, frowning when she saw me.

"Arm went to sleep," I said, smiling a little maniacally. I noticed she stayed close to the wall as she passed me. Maybe I should have told her I was an orchestra conductor doing my daily exercises instead.

"You're never going to have another sardine or a sardine cracker in your life if I don't see you right now," I said. It was an empty threat and the little tabby cat knew that.

We were approaching Melanie's office. Just then she stepped out into the hallway, smiling when she caught sight of me. "Hi, Kathleen," she said. "That was fast."

"Well, you know, cookies," I said.

Behind her Owen appeared, only for a few seconds, just long enough for me to see him walk into the office.

Melanie reached behind her and pulled the office door closed. She put her keys, which were on a bright blue lanyard, around her neck. "The chef's waiting for us in the kitchen," she said.

The cookies were delicious and very pretty—heart-shaped

with one side dipped in white chocolate—but they were also very crumbly.

"You're right," I said. I had crumbs on my fingers and the front of my sweater. "They're too messy for the library." *And for Patricia with all those quilts around,* I added silently. "Can you give me until morning before you call Patricia?" I asked Melanie. "I may have an idea to offer her that will work better."

She brushed a couple of stray crumbs from her violet-colored blouse. "Gladly." Her phone pinged then. She read what was on the screen and sighed. "I'm sorry, Kathleen," she said. "It seems we have a couple of disgruntled guests in one of our luxury suites."

I still had half a cookie in my hand. "Go take care of it. I can find my way back to the lobby."

She thanked me again for coming. I told her I'd talk to her sometime after lunch, and she left.

I thanked the chef for his help, retraced our steps all the way to the lobby, then waited a moment until both staff members at the front desk were busy with customers and headed down the corridor that led to Melanie's office. I had a furry trespasser to pick up. I walked like I belonged and no one stopped me.

When I tried to open Melanie's office door it was locked. It must have locked when she closed it. Now what was I going to do? I jiggled the handle and from inside heard an answering meow. I had to get Owen out before Melanie came back or someone caught me lurking there.

She hadn't set the touchpad lock when we'd gone to try the cookies so all I had to do was get the actual door lock open. I looked at the six-panel wooden door and realized the lockset was like the one on the door to the tai chi studio. I remembered what Milo had done to show Maggie how inadequate the lock was on the studio door. Would that trick work here? I didn't have a better option.

I fished my library card out of my wallet and slipped it into the crack between the door and the frame. It took two tries but I got the latch open.

I slipped inside, using the flashlight app on my phone so I could see what I was doing. I found Owen perched on the leather chair in the corner.

I glared at him. "What are you doing?"

He blinked at me and his nose twitched.

I had no idea why he'd wanted to get inside Melanie's office other than he knew I didn't want him there. I brushed at the gray-and-red blanket, hoping he hadn't gotten any cat hair on it.

There really was nothing that should have caught his attention: the old desk, the photo of the Riverwalk, one of the calendars that he and Hercules had posed for, the tiny plaque with the words "Valor, Truth, Honor." Just typical things you'd find in most offices. I reached for the cat and heard a noise outside in the corridor. We were caught. Well, I was caught. Owen could just disappear again.

I closed my eyes for a moment. When Melanie opened the

door I'd simply tell her that I came back to leave her a note and got stuck in her office. It was embarrassing, but not the end of the world.

Then I heard the beep of the digital lock and realized that Melanie wasn't coming in. She was just locking the door.

I bolted across the small space. "Hello? Hello?" I called out, banging on the door with the flat of my hand. "Melanie! Hello?"

Nothing.

She was gone. She hadn't heard me. Now what? I pounded on the door again. "Hello? Is anyone out there?"

No one came.

I made my way back to the chair and sat down. Okay, I'd just call Melanie instead, tell her my leaving a note story and get her to come let me out. Slightly more embarrassing but not by much.

There was no signal.

I rubbed the space between my eyes with the heel of my hand, remembering Melanie telling me she kept her office door wide open because the stone and concrete in this temporary office tended to disrupt the cell signal.

It seemed to be getting stuffier in the small space. Owen nuzzled my chin. "Okay, this isn't a big deal," I said. "I'll just use the phone on Melanie's desk to call her." I took a couple of deep breaths. It was definitely getting stuffier.

I made my way over to the desk, using my phone like a flashlight in one hand and carrying Owen with the other. I

207

tried to push what Melanie had said the other day about the phone in her office out of my mind: *Some days I have a landline and some I don't.*

I picked up the receiver. Today was a don't.

My heart raced. This couldn't be happening. I leaned against the edge of the desk, consciously breathing more slowly, willing my heart rate to slow down. I had a crazy sensation that I was going to use up all the air in the room if I didn't stop breathing so rapidly.

My knees were shaking and I slid off onto the floor. I was stuck inside this tiny office with no windows, stuck inside a space that was really the bottom of a closed-off ventilation shaft. My chest tightened and I couldn't get any air. I pressed my free hand to my chest and took several shaky breaths. I really didn't like small spaces.

Owen rubbed his face against my cheek, reminding me that I wasn't all alone, reminding me that we'd been in worse situations and gotten out. I swallowed a couple of times and wrapped both arms around him. "Okay, what do we do?" I said.

Owen wriggled out of my grasp. I tried to grab him but he was too fast. He was already prowling around Melanie's desk. "Forget it," I told him. "There's no secret passageway out of here. This *is* the secret passageway."

He ignored me, moved round the desk and put a paw on the brass grate on the wall. He looked over his shoulder at me. "Merow," he said. Was he trying to suggest a way out?

I nodded slowly. "Maybe."

I remembered Melanie saying the ventilation shaft was made of brick. It was old and maybe worn and uneven enough to climb. I felt like we were running out of air even though logically I knew that wasn't the case. I knew I either had to climb out or spend the night in the office. Pounding on the door and yelling wasn't going to help. What were the chances anyone would be in this part of the hotel for the rest of the night?

I looked at my phone again. I still had no cell service, not surprising considering I was at the bottom of an old ventilation shaft. The thought of spending all night in that room left me on the edge of panic. Climb it was.

I used the multipurpose tool on my key ring and got the brass grate loose on one side. The opening wasn't very big but it was big enough.

"You first," I said to Owen.

He peered into the darkness and then looked at me. He seemed doubtful.

"We're kind of out of options," I said. I shined my phone into the hole and Owen stepped through. I followed him.

Since we were at the bottom of the ventilation shaft there was a floor to stand on. The space was very, very dark even with the light from my phone. I forced myself to take slow breaths. I never should have gotten involved in Marcus's case. I should have checked the truck seat because I knew how much Owen liked stowing away. I bent down, picked him up and stuffed him inside my jacket, zippering it almost closed so that just his furry head was poking out.

"This is my fault," I said. "I'm the person. You're the cat. I'm the one who is supposed to know better."

"Mrr," he said.

"We're going to get out of this. We got out of that cabin before it exploded and we're getting out of here. And this is the last time I am ever getting stuck in a small space. From now on we're only going into big cavernous areas. Canyons, hockey rinks, airplane hangars." I knew I was rambling but it helped distract me from panicking.

The shaft was maybe four feet square, no more. I put my hands out and felt the brick sides. The brick was in much better shape than I'd expected. I didn't feel any place that I could get a handhold. And then my hand touched something cold and smooth. Metal. I shone the light up and there it was, a ladder mounted flush to the side wall. It must have been something workmen had used to maintain the tunnel. It could be close to a hundred years old. I took hold of the bottom of the ladder with both hands and pulled. It seemed to be fixed securely to the brick.

We could get out.

"You can do this, Katydid," I could hear my mom say in my head. "Stiffen the sinews, summon up the blood."

I gave one more yank on the bottom rung of the ladder. It didn't move.

"Hang on," I said to Owen. I reached for the highest rung I could grab and pulled myself up. The ladder held. I started to climb.

Because I needed both hands, my phone was in my pocket and I had no light. It was the darkest place I'd ever been in, but eventually up above me I saw a tiny glimmer of reflected light. A way out?

I was wheezing. My arms and shoulders burned. I was doing more pulling myself up the rungs than climbing. As I made my way up, I realized the faint bit of light I could see was coming from another grate-covered opening to my right. I was guessing we were about level with the floor above Melanie's temporary office. This had to be a way out.

I leaned sideways for a better look. Was that one of the rooms that were being renovated? And how was I going to get the grate off the hole in the wall?

I pulled myself up until my feet were level with the grate. I eased Owen more to my left side. "Almost out," I told him. I felt his cold nose on my neck.

I moved as far to the right of the ladder as I could, holding on with my left hand and bracing my right hand on the brick above the grate. Then I lifted my foot off the ladder and kicked the grate.

It gave just a little. I waited, listening, hoping maybe somebody would hear me and come to investigate.

Silence.

It took three more kicks but the grate finally fell back into the room. Now all I had to do was shift ninety degrees and reach that opening.

I felt around in the darkness with my foot and found a small foothold, a break in the mortar around two bricks. For a moment it would have to hold all my body weight.

I took hold of the right side of the opening with my right hand, stretching as far as I could. I wedged my foot against the brick. I thought of tai chi, moving fluidly from one movement to the next.

I took a breath.

I let it out.

I moved.

I grabbed the left side of the shaft with my other hand. For a moment I teetered there and then I moved my other foot over, ducked my head and shoulders into the cramped opening and threw my weight forward, rolling to my right side as I did to protect Owen. My right foot slid off its foothold but enough of my body was inside that I didn't fall.

For a moment I just lay there, half of me in the opening and half of me out, trying not to throw up. Owen wriggled out of the top of my jacket and shook himself. He licked my chin.

"We're all right," I wheezed.

After a couple of minutes I pulled my legs into the room and sat up. There was construction debris all around us. We were in what was probably going to be the men's bathroom. A urinal lay on its side next to me. I started to laugh as much from relief as anything else. This was probably the stupidest thing I'd ever done, but we'd made it.

I got to my feet and replaced the grate by propping it against the wall. I brushed as much dirt and dust off of myself as I could.

I wasn't wasting any more time in the room. I wanted to be outside, where there was lots of fresh air to breathe and lots of space.

I stepped into the corridor. Owen wriggled out of my grasp and walked down the middle of the hallway as though he were a guest.

"Great. Now you want the whole world to see you," I said. Somehow he knew that now I wanted him to vanish so he wasn't going to do it.

I heard voices. "Half a sardine," I said in desperation. His left ear twitched but he kept walking, both of which I could see because he was still visible.

I took two long steps, leaned forward and swept him up just as a man and woman came around the corner. I smiled pleasantly and said "Good evening" as we passed each other.

Owen squirmed but I had a good grip on him this time. I made it to one of the side doors, went down a flight of stairs and stepped outside. For a moment I just stood in the parking lot taking deep breaths of cool, fresh air. Finally, I speed-walked to the truck, where I deposited Owen on the seat. He refused to look at me.

I leaned sideways. "Next time take the half a sardine," I told him.

Owen sulked as I pulled out of the parking lot and headed for home. He continued his pout as we drove up Mountain Road. I pictured Melanie's office. I hoped I'd gotten any cat hair Owen may have left on the scarlet-and-gray blanket.

"Scarlet and gray," I said aloud. From the corner of my eye I saw the cat finally look at me. "Those are the colors of Saint Edwin University."

I pictured the school seal in one of the magazines Burtis had loaned me and the Latin words on it: "Virtus, Veritas, Honestas." Valor, Truth, Honor. Gray background. Red lettering.

"Melanie Davis went to Saint Edwin University," I said slowly. There was no other logical explanation for the woven blanket and the plaque on the wall. Melanie had told me she had worked with Wallace briefly but she barely knew him. She hadn't said they'd gone to the same college. Coincidence? Lewis Wallace died in the hotel she managed. There was no way *that* was a coincidence. It had to mean something. The question was, what?

chapter 13

I didn't know what to do with what I had figured out. Did I call Marcus? Did I turn around, drive back down the hill and confront Melanie? I knew that Marcus would say the fact that Melanie Davis went to the same university as Lewis Wallace didn't necessarily mean anything—assuming I was right about that, and I was certain that I was. Even though it was a small campus, there could be hundreds or thousands of students in a given year. Melanie and Lewis Wallace could have both gone to Saint Edwin and never met. But it felt like too much of a coincidence to me. I'd heard Burtis quote Yogi Berra on that subject: *"That's too coincidental to be a coincidence."* Made sense to me.

But if I went to talk to Melanie, what would I say? "I think you went to the same college as Lewis Wallace. I think you knew him better than you're letting on and I think you may have a connection to his death." I needed more than that.

I parked in the driveway and climbed out of the truck. Owen jumped down and headed for the back door.

I let him into the house and he went directly to sit in front of the cupboard where I kept the sardines. He stared at me. I folded my arms and stared back.

"Mrr," he said.

"Why do you think you deserve a sardine?" I asked. "You snuck into the truck, you snuck into the hotel and you snuck into Melanie's office. That's a lot of sneaking. And I had to climb up a ventilation shaft. In the dark." I brushed dirt off the right arm of my jacket. "Carrying you, by the way."

He swiped a paw over his face.

I nodded. "Yes, I concede that you are very cute, but that has nothing to do with you getting a sardine. What else do you have?"

He continued to stare at me without a meow or a murp or a grumble as though the reason should be obvious. I knew that if he hadn't snuck into the truck and the hotel and then into Melanie's office I might not have made the connection that Melanie and Lewis Wallace likely knew each other better than she was letting on. Or at least it would have taken a lot longer. I could have done with not having to climb my way up that narrow brick shaft, though that was on me, not the cat.

It seemed Owen knew that, too. I got out a can of sardines and gave him part of one without comment.

He was just finishing eating it when Ethan came in.

"How far did you walk?" I asked.

He swept a hand over his hair. "I didn't exactly walk very far. I've been over talking to Rebecca."

That and eating pie, I suspected. His teeth looked a little blue.

He yawned and stretched both arms over his head. "So what were you doing? Did you just come from somewhere?"

My keys were on the table.

"I had to deal with a cookie emergency," I said.

"As in we don't have any?"

"No. As in I need about a hundred and fifty for the quilt festival at the library."

He opened the fridge door and peered inside. "No offense, but just about everything they do in this town has food associated with it."

I laughed. "You're right. It's the unofficial town motto: We have cookies."

I left Ethan making a peanut butter and jelly sandwich with a small, furry supervisor. I went into the living room and called Susan, explaining the cookie problem.

"Do you think Eric would be able to make his new maple cookies for the opening of the festival?"

"Crappy timing, Kathleen," she said. "He's catering the regional tourism coalition's breakfast that day. There's no way he could get all those cookies made and they won't have the right texture if he makes them in advance and freezes them."

I exhaled loudly. So much for my solution to the cookie problem.

"Hang on, though," Susan continued. "I think there's a chance he would be willing to share his recipe for the cookies with the chef at the St. James. All of Eric's recipes can stand up to being doubled or tripled."

"That would work, as long as Eric feels comfortable with someone else using his recipe. Please tell him he doesn't have to say yes."

"I'll tell him," she said, "but I'm pretty sure he will say yes. I'll let you know in the morning."

I thanked her and said good night.

It wasn't that late but there wasn't anything else I could do about the cookies or Melanie or talking to Marcus about the cats.

I poked my head around the kitchen doorway. "I'm going to take a bath," I said to Ethan. Owen had disappeared. Not literally, I hoped.

"You mind if I play a bit?" he asked.

I shook my head. "Go ahead. I'll see you in the morning."

I filled the tub with hot water and one of Maggie's herbal bath remedies for achy muscles. I wasn't sure I was going to be able to lift my arms over my head in the morning.

The sound of Ethan's guitar playing floated up from downstairs. It had been a long time since I'd listened to him play like this, without having to share the music with anyone else.

Hercules was stretched out on the bath mat. "I hate that he's going home in a few days," I said.

The cat gave a soft murp of sympathy.

I leaned my head back and closed my eyes. I was going to do a Scarlett O'Hara and think about that—and everything else—tomorrow.

Susan arrived for her shift in the morning with a copy of the cookie recipe. "Eric said—and this is a direct quote—'Tell Kathleen I have worked with Patricia Queen before. Here is the recipe, with my sympathy.'"

"Thank you and Eric," I said, giving her a hug. "And for the record, Patricia isn't really that difficult."

Susan nudged her cat's-eye glasses up her nose. "Kathleen, she reminded you to clean the screens of all of our computers the week of the festival so there would be no unsightly fingerprints." She said the last few words in perfect mimicry of Patricia. "The only reason that wasn't a problem is because *you* would have done that anyway!"

I felt my face get red as Susan laughed.

"Seriously," I said. "I owe both of you. How about I babysit the boys so you and Eric can go out?"

Susan regarded me with a fair amount of skepticism, one

hand on her hip. "Are you insane? Not that I'm *not* taking you up on the offer."

I assured her about my mental health and the genuineness of my offer to watch the boys. She headed up to get coffee.

Just before lunch I called Melanie and explained about the maple cookies and how I had Eric's recipe for the St. James chef to use with Eric's permission. "The cookies are traditional enough for Patricia, with enough of a different twist for people to remark on them—and I've already cleared the change with Patricia."

Melanie thanked me profusely. "I owe you," she said. "A kidney, help moving, I'm your woman."

I wondered what she'd say if I just asked her for the truth about Lewis Wallace.

Marcus stopped by with lunch about quarter after twelve. "How did you know I forgot mine?" I asked.

"I talked to your brother." He handed me a brown paper bag. "Meatloaf sandwich from Fern's with a chopped apple and carrot salad on the side."

My stomach growled in appreciation. "Where did you see Ethan?" I asked.

"He was at the co-op store. He and his friends are putting a couple of new locks on the doors."

Ethan was still trying to make points with Maggie. Hearing about the door reminded me that I needed to tell Marcus what I'd figured out about Melanie. I left out the part about crawling up the ventilation shaft. My shoulders still ached.

Marcus made a face. "Why would she lie about something like that? She admitted she knew the man. Why not just say they knew each other in college?"

"I don't know," I said. "Wallace played football. A lot of people would have known who he was. And I think if she'd wanted to kill the man she wouldn't have done it in her own hotel. So why keep that secret?"

"People have done a lot stupider things than that," he said.

"Wallace struggled with the person who killed him." I gestured with the bag holding my lunch. "It couldn't have been Melanie. He must have had a hundred and fifty pounds on her."

"Not so fast," Marcus said. "Wallace was bigger, but he was more fat than muscle and he had asthma. Plus, he was having a reaction to the peanut butter. Melanie Davis is in much better shape. She runs and she boxes. In theory she could have killed him."

The question was, had she?

When I got to class that evening Maggie and Roma were standing by the tea table talking. Maggie was smiling and gesturing with one hand. Whatever the topic of conversation was it seemed to be making her happy.

I walked over to join them. "Hi," I said.

Roma smiled. "Hi," she said. "I'm supposed to tell you volume nine. Sydney said that would mean something to you."

I nodded. "It does. We're both reading a young adult fantasy series that has fourteen books. Syd is now officially ahead of me." I smiled. "We've been imagining the books turned into a movie and e-mailing each other our picks for the cast."

"Thank you for encouraging her," Roma said.

"First of all, she's a great kid. And second, I'm happy to have someone to talk about the books with. No one else I know has been reading them."

Maggie took a sip of her tea, which smelled like cranberries and honey, and set her mug on the table. "Roma suggested we all go out to Wisteria Hill Friday night. I know Ethan is leaving on Saturday. Do you have anything planned?"

I shook my head. "I don't. And Ethan didn't mention any plans to me."

"Then it's settled," Maggie said. "I'll make pizza."

I looked at Roma. "Then I'll do the dishes." I gave her a hug. "Thank you," I said. "I'm looking forward to it." It would be good not to think about Lewis Wallace for a change.

I was changing my shoes after class when Rebecca came and sat next to me.

"Are you having any luck figuring out who might have killed Mr. Wallace?" she asked.

"Not really," I said.

Her expression softened. "I'm going to share a little secret with you, Kathleen. I'm not anywhere close to being as skilled as you are at using a computer to find things out, but I've met a lot of people in my life. That happens when you're a hairdresser." She smiled. "So I have my own way of learning things."

I knew that was true. Rebecca was genuinely interested in people.

"And Everett does business with a lot of different people, which means I've had the opportunity to get to know many people's staff members, the people who know where the bodies are buried, so to speak. After you came over, I wanted to learn a little bit more about Lewis Wallace. I'd heard a lot of negative things. I wanted to know if anyone had anything positive to say."

"Did they?" I asked. She answered my question with a question of her own.

"Did you know that Lewis Wallace lost both of his parents when he was barely an adult?"

I nodded. "I did." I pulled on my left boot and started to tighten the laces.

"Did you know his mother died from a very aggressive brain tumor?"

"I didn't know that," I said. I couldn't help feeling a twinge of sympathy for Wallace. What had it been like to watch his mother die that way?

Rebecca folded her hands in her lap. "Two months ago, Mr. Wallace made a substantial donation to a group that's doing research into brain cancer, into the type of brain cancer that killed his mother. No fanfare, Kathleen. No public acknowledgment. Just money to fund research that someday might save someone else's mother."

It was the last thing I'd expected her to tell me.

Rebecca patted my arm. "Most people are not all one thing," she said. "You might want to keep that in mind."

"I will," I said.

She smiled then. "I had a lovely visit with your brother yesterday. He showed me some delightful pictures of you." Her eyes twinkled.

"I'm going to kill him," I said matter-of-factly, gesturing with the boot I was holding. "No. Marcus is too good a detective. He'll figure it out. I'm going to wait until Ethan's asleep and shave his head."

For Ethan that would be a fate worse than death.

Rebecca put her shoes in her canvas bag. "Don't give your brother a hard time, now. I'm the one who asked if he had any photos of you when you were a child." She gave me a sideways glance. "I didn't know you knew how to twirl a baton."

I sent her a daggers look. "That settles it. I'm not going to just shave his head. I'm going to shave every part of his body."

Rebecca stood up and pulled on her jacket. "You were adorable."

"I almost burned down my elementary school. Who thought it was a good idea to let an eight-year-old twirl a baton that was on fire?" I laughed in spite of myself. "My mother had to draw on my eyebrows for the next two months."

She reached down and gave my shoulder a squeeze. "I still

think you were adorable. With or without eyebrows." She started down the stairs. "If you shave Ethan's head make sure you stroke the razor in the direction of the hair growth," she said over her shoulder. "You wouldn't want him to end up with a rash."

I pulled on my other boot, stuffed my towel and shoes into my backpack and grabbed my jacket. I'd found a parking space right out front. I slid behind the wheel and looked down the street in the direction of the hotel. I could just walk down there, see if Melanie was still around and ask her what her connection to Lewis Wallace was. I sat there for a minute or so, trying to come up with a good reason not to. But I couldn't.

Melanie was in her office. She put in a lot of long days. Once again, the desk clerk directed me across the lobby and down the hall. The office door was wide open as before, and I knocked on the jamb. She looked up in surprise. "Hi, Kathleen," she said. "Did we have a meeting I forgot about?"

"No," I said. I hesitated. My mother had an expression; in for a penny, in for a pound. She'd learned it from a British wardrobe mistress and could quote the words using the woman's precise British accent. I could hear her voice in my head now.

I gestured at the woven blanket still tossed over the arm of the leather chair. "I know you went to Saint Edwin University. You and Lewis Wallace were friends in college."

The color drained from Melanie's face. She swallowed. "No, we weren't."

I didn't say anything. I just looked at her.

Her mouth worked. Her eyes slipped away from mine. "I should have guessed you'd come to see me. Detective Gordon was here earlier today." She cleared her throat. "Lew and I weren't friends. I was his tutor for a couple of his classes. He was failing pretty much everything, mostly because he was lazy and entitled. On the field he was fast and strong, the proverbial immovable object. He didn't see the point in studying. He thought the rule that he had to maintain a minimum grade point average was stupid. He knew how much the team needed him. He thought it was going to be his ticket to the big time. Turned out he was wrong."

"He was accused of cheating."

Melanie stared at me for a moment. "Yes, but he was cleared of all that. Like I said, Lew was mostly lazy—at least off of the football field."

"How did you end up working together?" I asked.

"That was just chance. I didn't stay at the job very long. I could see that the company was only headed down."

"He wanted your support for the deal he was pitching to the town." It was a guess but a good one it turns out.

She smoothed her hair with one hand. "I told him I couldn't get involved because I worked for the hotel and they had a policy about that sort of thing."

"Is that true?"

Melanie shook her head. "Not specifically, no. I didn't want to get involved because I wasn't sure the deal was going to work. I know what kind of a student he was and that his first business failed."

"You didn't think that he'd changed," I said.

"I just wasn't convinced he had what it took to run a successful business." She looked away again.

"You admitted you knew Wallace. Why wouldn't you say the two of you went to college together?"

"Lew asked me to keep that quiet. He said most people didn't care if you had a business that went under. It happens all the time. But he said that anytime someone found out that he'd been suspected of cheating back in college they got antsy, even though he was cleared. Two other students were expelled; one for using the stolen answers and one for stealing them." She sighed softly. "I agreed, partly because all those years ago, with that cheating business, I was questioned, too. I had nothing to do with any of it and no one ever said I did, but I want to move up in this company. Maybe I was overreacting, but I know how people think: Where there's smoke there's fire. So I said yes."

I believed her.

She got to her feet. "For what it's worth, I know it was stupid of me in the first place to keep the fact that Lew and I knew each other in college a secret. And I just made things worse when I didn't say anything after he was killed." Her gaze slid away from mine again.

I believed her as far as her explanation went but I also knew she wasn't telling me everything. That much was clear from the way she had trouble keeping eye contact. But the conversation seemed to have gone as far as it was going to for the moment. I thanked her for talking to me and headed back toward the lobby.

I was almost to the front entrance when I remembered that I had downloaded a photo of Zach Redmond onto my phone because I'd intended to ask Melanie if any of the staff might have seen him the night Lewis Wallace died. Should I go back to her office? Before I could decide I bumped into someone. My phone landed on the floor. "I'm sorry," the young man said. Then he smiled. "Hey, Ms. Paulson."

I smiled back. "Hi, Levi." Levi Ericson worked part-time as a waiter at the St. James. He was a voracious reader, at the library at least once and often twice a week.

Levi bent down and picked up my phone, automatically glancing at the screen as he did. "Hey, is this guy a friend of yours?" he asked.

"Sort of," I said as he handed my cell back to me.

"That is so great. See, the thing is, he was in here last week wearing a 1987 Guns N' Roses T-shirt for their Appetite for Destruction European tour. That shirt is a collector's item worth more than a thousand dollars. I'd kinda like to know where he got it."

"He was here?" I pointed at my phone screen. "This man? You're sure?"

Levi nodded. "Oh yeah. Like I said, collectors would spend a lot for that shirt."

"Do you remember what day it was?" Mentally I crossed my fingers.

"Well, it could only be last Saturday night because that's the only time I worked last week."

Last Saturday night. The night of the murder.

I realized Levi was looking at me, a frown knotting between his eyebrows. "He's a . . . a friend of a friend," I said. "But I'll ask about the shirt if I get the chance."

Levi thanked me and headed for the back of the hotel.

I still had more questions than answers. I did think Melanie had told me the truth. I just didn't think she'd told me all of it. And now I knew that Zach had been at the hotel the night of the murder. I'd gone from no suspects to possibly two. Now what?

chapter 14

My mind was racing and I knew there was no way I was going to be able to sleep for a while. I couldn't think of anything I could do with respect to what I'd learned about Zach, or the fact that I still believed Melanie was hiding something, but I could do more digging into Lewis Wallace.

I sat in the middle of my bed and read the last article from the third of Burtis's magazines. It was a follow-up to the piece they had done on a group of freshman players four years earlier. I didn't learn anything new from the few paragraphs about Lewis Wallace but there was a photo of twenty-two-year-old Wallace and his Canadian fiancée, Julie Kendall.

Hercules had wandered in at one point and was sprawled out on my shoe.

I remembered that Melanie had mentioned Lewis Wallace might have been married briefly during his CFL playing days. "Would Julie Kendall have any reason to want her ex-husband dead?" I asked the cat.

His whiskers twitched. "Merow," he said.

Maybe.

I stood up, stretched and headed for the bathroom to brush my teeth. Hercules followed me.

"What is Melanie still hiding?" I asked him around a mouth of toothpaste. "Whatever it is has to be connected to her and Wallace's college days. Do you think they could have been mixed up in that cheating business somehow?" It seemed like a weak reason to kill someone.

I yawned and the cat did as well. "I don't know," I said with a sigh. "Maybe I'm wrong thinking Melanie did anything. Maybe it's Zach. Maybe it was a Romulan."

It was a busy Wednesday at the library and I didn't really have any time to think about Melanie, Zach or rogue Romulans. Ethan and the guys were going to a concert at the high school that evening at the invitation of Ruby.

"I didn't know you liked band music," I said to Ethan. I had a feeling the music wasn't the reason they were going.

"They have a jazz band," Ethan said. "Your friend Ruby said I should definitely hear the drummer."

Derek smirked. "And Milo thinks your friend Ruby is cute."

That pretty much explained everything.

One of Marcus's former colleagues on the police force was in town and some of the guys were going out with him. Marcus was going to be the designated driver. He stopped in on his way out to The Brick.

"I feel like I've barely seen you in the last week between this case and the one that's on trial, plus all the extra hockey practices." The high school girl's hockey team had advanced to the state final. He wrapped his arms around me as we stood in the porch.

"I know," I said. "I'm so happy to have had all this time with Ethan and I'm going to miss him like crazy when he leaves, but I do miss seeing you." I kissed him and over his shoulder Owen winked into view on the bench where Hercules usually sat.

"I'll talk to you tomorrow," he said as he let me go and turned around. He started at the sight of Owen, sitting there with his head cocked to one side in seemingly innocent curiosity, looking at me.

"I walked right by Owen and didn't even see him." He gave his head a shake. "I think I really should get my eyes checked."

"Maybe when this case is over," I said. That seemed to be my answer to a lot of things.

SOFIE KELLY

Owen continued to eye me even after Marcus was gone.

"I'm going to tell him," I said, a little more sharply than I'd intended.

Owen gave what sounded like a snort of derision and disappeared again.

The house seemed too quiet and I was at loose ends. I took some muffins out of the freezer. I brushed off my boots. I vacuumed cat hair off the stairs. Finally, I got out my laptop and sat on the sofa in the living room.

Zach Redmond was everywhere on social media. He liked action movies, spicy Buffalo wings and rock climbing if the pictures he posted were any indication. And he was working.

I could drive up to The Brick, I realized. I could talk to him. I could get some answers.

The place was quiet when I got there. Zach looked up and smiled as I approached the bar. I ordered ginger ale and a plate of onion rings. The rings were almost as good as the fries.

"So what are you doing here on a Wednesday night all by yourself?" he asked with that pretty-boy smile. "Not that I'm complaining."

"I wanted to ask you a question," I said.

"If you're asking for my phone number or a piece of my heart you can have both," he said, pressing one hand to his chest.

His flirting was so obvious I laughed in spite of myself. Zach could be charming in a clueless-little-boy way.

"You saw the altercation between Lewis Wallace and my

friend," I said. "The other night when I was here you said something about karma catching up with Wallace. What did you mean?"

At first he didn't say anything. I waited, knowing most people didn't like the silence and would end up saying something to fill it.

"Aww, what the hell. I guess there's no point in keeping it a secret now. I've already told the cops. Wallace was about to be investigated by the Securities and Exchange Commission. I had copies of a lot of the paperwork from my grandfather's business. I gave them pretty much everything, and that, along with a bunch of other stuff, was pretty much going to put Wallace out of business and behind bars in an orange jumpsuit."

"Redmond Signs was your grandfather's business," I said. "In Red Wing."

He nodded. "Yeah, Wallace and his buddies put it out of business."

"Why were you at the hotel the night he died?"

He looked away. I was afraid he was going to walk away as well. I put a hand on his arm to keep him there and waited.

"I went because I wanted to gloat that he was going to be brought down," he finally said. "But I didn't talk to him."

I frowned. "What do you mean? He wasn't there?"

Zach shook his head. "Oh, he was there. He was standing in one of the hallways arguing with someone. I couldn't see who it was and I didn't hear the other person talk." He'd been looking down but now he met my gaze head-on. "I didn't kill him if that's what you think. I left then. I realized how stupid what I'd been going to do was. He was alive when I left and I have an alibi for after that." He cleared his throat. "There's this girl I've seen a few times. I was with her." His eyes flicked away for a moment and then came back. "At church. She volunteers overnight a couple of times a month at the shelter they run."

Church. Zach had been at church. That alibi was just far-fetched enough to be true.

I spent a few minutes at lunchtime on the computer trying to track down Lewis Wallace's ex-wife, Julie Kendall. I didn't have much luck. I had no idea if she was still in the Montreal area or somewhere else in Canada. I wasn't even sure what last name she was using. For all I knew she could have remarried. There had to be a better way of finding her.

Mary walked by my door carrying a stapler. An idea began to spin in my mind. I shut off the computer and went downstairs.

I found Mary at the front desk stapling a report for a slightly panicked teenage boy. "There," she said. "Next time don't leave things until the last minute."

"Yes, Mrs. Lowe," the boy said. Then he jammed the paper in his backpack and headed for the door.

Mary shook her head and turned to me. "I'm trying not to think about the fact that someday that child will be running the world." She smiled. "What can I do for you?"

"I have a proposition for Bridget."

"And you want me to put in a good word for you?"

"I was actually hoping you'd get her on the phone so I wouldn't have to go through her assistant."

I waited for Mary to ask what my proposition was, but she didn't. Instead she reached for the phone. "Hi, kiddo," she said when Bridget answered. "I'm with Kathleen and she has a proposal for you. I think you should listen to her." She handed me the phone.

"Hello, Bridget," I said.

"Hi, Kathleen," she replied. "Mom says you want to talk to me about something?"

I braced one hand against the counter. "I do. I know you must be digging into Lewis Wallace's background. Did you know he had an ex-wife?"

"No, I didn't," she said.

I'd been counting on that. The *Mayville Heights Chronicle* may have been an award-winning newspaper but like most papers these days it had to do more with less. Without Burtis's magazines I wouldn't have known Julie Kendall's name.

"How would you like her name along with the name of the last city I can confirm she lived in?"

"What's in it for you?" Like her mother, Bridget was direct.

"I know you have a source connected with the police department, so I know you'll be able to get this information eventually. I'm giving you a way to get it now. In return, all I want is the woman's contact information. You have sources I don't. You can find her a lot faster than I can."

"What's her name?"

"We have a deal?" I asked.

"We have a deal," Bridget said.

I gave her Julie Kendall's name and my cell number.

"I'll be in touch," she said.

I ended the call and handed the phone back to Mary.

"Does Marcus know about this?" she said. "Or is this don't ask, don't tell?"

"If he asks, I'll tell," I said. I was really hoping he didn't ask.

The text came at four thirty. Just a phone number. Since I was still at work I decided to wait until after supper to call it.

I stopped at the St. James on my way home. Melanie had called. The chef had made a test batch of Eric's maple cookies. She wanted me to try one before she called Patricia. It had been the kind of day that would benefit from having a cookie or two added to it, so I said yes.

Eric's maple leaf cookies had turned out perfectly—thin and crisp but not crumbly and with just a hint of maple sweetness.

"These are delicious," I said.

"According to the chef, it's the recipe," Melanie said. "Please thank Eric again."

I nodded. "I will." I picked up my bag and was about to leave, but something made me stop. Some instinct, maybe?

"You helped him cheat," I blurted.

"I already told you," she said, a tinge of annoyance in her voice. "I didn't have anything to do with stealing those tests." Her shoulders were rigid.

"I believe you," I said. "But you did help Wallace get his marks up, and it wasn't by tutoring him."

Silence hung between us like smoke in the air. I didn't need her confirmation. The look on her face was enough.

She put both hands flat on the top of her desk as though bracing herself for whatever was coming. "What I told you before about not wanting to jeopardize my chances of moving up in this business by having that old scandal come up was true."

I nodded but didn't say anything.

"There was a lot more to it. I *didn't* help Lew steal those tests. That's the truth. And I didn't know for a long time that he had."

"But you did help him cheat in some way, didn't you?" I said.

"Yes. I did his assignments. Not perfectly, mind you; no one would have believed that. I just did them well enough to get his class average up." She slid her right hand over the desktop as though she was feeling for blemishes on the wooden surface.

"And the university suspected."

She nodded. "Suspected but never proved. I needed the money, Kathleen. It sounds like an excuse because, well, it is. And it's the biggest mistake I ever made. I should have gotten a job waiting tables or selling my blood. Anything would have been better. That one mistake has been following me around for twenty years."

I studied her across the desk. Nothing in her body language or her tone suggested she was being anything less than one hundred percent truthful. "Was it just chance that Wallace decided to approach the town about setting up his business? Or was it because you were here?"

"He was looking at the state in general because there were some tax breaks for a new business like his, but I think he chose Mayville Heights because he'd discovered I worked here. He told me he saw a magazine article about me when he was flying home from somewhere. It was one of those inspiring up-from-nothing pieces that I probably shouldn't have agreed to." She rubbed her left temple as though she had a headache.

"Wallace was blackmailing you."

Melanie shook her head. "No. Believe it or not, he considered us friends. As far as he was concerned, friends help one another out."

"Did you help him?"

"At first I said no."

"So what changed?"

She leaned back in her chair and her expression turned thoughtful. "In a way, I guess he did."

I narrowed my gaze at her. "You've lost me," I said.

"The second night he was here, I was working late and as usual Lew was up wandering around. He walked by the office, saw me and we started talking, really talking. Lew was trying to fix things in his life. He'd connected with his mother's family. They were good people from the way he spoke about them and it seemed to inspire him to make some changes." She smiled. "I think there was a lot of one step forward and two steps back. He's always thought he was God's gift to women and from what I could see he couldn't seem to get it through his head that he wasn't. But he said he was trying to fix his mistakes."

That explained his settling the lawsuits.

"I told him I thought we should come clean and just take the consequences. He said he had more to lose than I did."

"He took those tests."

She nodded. "And paid someone else to take the blame. I'd always suspected he had. Lew said if he admitted he'd cheated it would destroy any chance of him having a second chance at football."

I frowned at her. "Wait a minute. A second chance at football?"

"Lew told me that he had a part-time job lined up as an assistant high school football coach, starting in the fall. I don't know if he would have been any good, but when he talked about it I could tell how much it meant to him. He swore that he was going to make the supplement business a success and use the money to do good things and become a successful coach and inspire young people. I told him that he would be stuck with the weight of that secret for the rest of his life."

"Sisyphus," I said.

Melanie made a face. "I'm sorry," she said. "I don't understand."

"Sisyphus was a king from Greek mythology. A pretty despicable guy. Zeus punished him for his treachery by forcing him to roll a huge boulder up a hill. Just before it reached the top it would roll down again. Sisyphus was left rolling that boulder up the hill for eternity."

Melanie nodded. "That's what those lies we told felt like to me: a big boulder that could flatten us both."

It was impossible not to feel some sympathy for her.

"I didn't kill him, Kathleen," she said. "I was upstairs in my old office drinking and writing my resignation letter when Lew died, and I can prove it." Her voice got a little stronger. "I Skyped my best friend in California and we talked for half the night. You can call her or the police can. You can check my computer."

I nodded. This time I *did* believe her.

chapter 15

There was no sign of the guys when I got home. No sign of Owen or Hercules, either. I checked my watch. I had time to call Julie Kendall.

I went upstairs and changed into my tai chi clothes. Then I picked up the phone and dialed Julie Kendall's number. A woman with just a hint of a French accent answered on the fourth ring.

"My name is Kathleen Paulson," I said.

"Bridget Lowe said you'd probably be calling." Julie had a warm, friendly voice. "You, uh, you found Lew."

I found myself nodding even though she couldn't see me. "I did . . . I'm sorry."

"Thank you," she said. "We've been divorced for a long time but I never wanted anything like this to happen to him. Even in my angriest moments."

"Do you mind if I ask when the last time you spoke to him was?"

"I hadn't heard from Lew in probably five years and then about three weeks ago, out of the blue, he called me, wanted to meet. He said he was going to be in Montreal in a couple of days and it was important. I was just curious enough to agree. We met at a coffee shop and he handed me a check."

I wasn't sure I'd heard her correctly. "A check?" I said. "He owed you money?"

"I would have told you no," Julie said. "Lew said it was money he should have given me when we divorced, my half of what I thought was a pretty much useless piece of property in Indiana of all places. I couldn't believe it."

"Did he tell you why he was doing this now?"

"He said he'd changed. Then he hit on our waitress." She laughed. "He may have changed but not completely. We talked for a while. He told me he'd made contact just by chance with a cousin on his mother's side of the family. I don't know if you know but he was just nineteen when his mother died. Anyway, they ended up getting together and he met the rest of the family—his mother's sisters and his cousins. She'd run off, it seemed, with his father and hadn't been in contact with them. Meeting them all, being welcomed by them all, did something to him. Something good."

I shifted on the bed, tucking one leg underneath me. "Do you happen to know if he was in touch with anyone else from his past?"

"I think he talked to Chunk," she said. "Dwayne Parker. They played together—college and pro."

Dwayne Parker. I leaned over and scribbled the name on the bottom of the grocery list that was on my nightstand. "They stayed in contact?"

"I'm not sure about that. All I can tell you is that Lew said Chunk was married and had five kids. But I got the feeling that they'd talked fairly recently."

"Do you have any idea how I could find Mr. Parker?" I asked.

"He's a football scout at Saint Edwin University," she said. "Lew said neither one of them could really get away from the place."

I thanked Julie for her time and promised I'd call her again when I had anything new to share.

"Lew could be an ass a lot of the time but he didn't deserve what happened to him," Julie said. "And I hate the thought that maybe, finally, he was starting to grow up and he lost the chance."

When I went downstairs I found Ethan in the living room playing his guitar for a furry audience of two. "Are Milo and Derek coming for supper?" I asked.

He shook his head. "They went to Red Wing to get that guitar of Milo's. They'll be back later."

"So it's just us."

He nodded.

"Do you want dumplings with your chicken soup or crackers?" I asked.

"Dumplings, please," he said with a grin. His enthusiasm was echoed by his audience.

All three of them followed me into the kitchen.

"Want me to set the table?" Ethan asked.

"Please," I said. I got out a mixing bowl and the measuring cups. The soup was in the refrigerator.

"Are you having any luck figuring out who killed that Wallace guy?" Ethan said.

I shook my head. "Not yet."

"Yeah, well the guy was a flaming bag of crap."

I swung around to look at him. "What?"

"C'mon, Kath, you know what I mean," he said, his voice casual. "The man was a sack of—"

"Stop," I said.

"Well, he was." He seemed taken aback by the forcefulness in my voice.

"Don't talk that way about someone, anyone."

"Why not?" It was impossible to miss the challenge in his voice now.

"Because . . . because most people are not all one thing," I said, repeating Rebecca's words to me. "They're not all good or all bad. They're not saint or sinner."

He gave a snort of contempt. "You were there for three run-ins with the guy. You're not going to try to tell me that Lewis Wallace was some kind of saint, are you?"

I sighed. "Of course not. But he wasn't some evil monster, either." And now I knew from both Melanie and Wallace's ex that the man had at least been trying to change. "You know, Lewis Wallace was barely an adult when both of his parents died. I don't want to think about who I would have turned out to be without Mom and Dad around."

I knew by the stubborn set to his jaw that he wasn't yielding anything to me.

"When you were nineteen were all your choices so perfect that you didn't need Mom and Dad?" I continued. "Are you really going to try and tell me that you don't need them now sometimes?"

"I never kicked a service dog."

I leaned against the counter. "You're right. And why is that? Because Thea Paulson is your mother. Because John Paulson is your father. They taught you better and when you screwed up—and you did, little brother, because we all do—they showed you how to do better the next time."

"You're just making excuses for the guy," Ethan said.

I shook my head, frustrated that he didn't seem to be getting my point. "No. I'm trying not to judge, and yes, I did a lot of that at first because the guy did act like a jerk every time I encountered him. Now I'm trying to figure out who Lewis

Wallace really was so maybe that will help me figure out how he ended up dead in that meeting room, *which, by the way,* is something you asked me to do."

I turned back around and reached for the flour.

"I'm sorry," Ethan said.

I wasn't sure if he meant he was sorry for calling Lewis Wallace a flaming bag of crap or for asking me to figure out who'd killed the man.

I decided for now I was happier not knowing.

🐾

I went to tai chi class but my focus wasn't really on the class.

"Is everything all right?" Maggie asked at the end of class as I used the edge of my T-shirt to blot my sweaty face because I'd forgotten my towel.

"I'm just tired," I said. "Owen decided that quarter to six was the perfect time to get up this morning." After meowing in my ear hadn't worked the cat had batted my face with one paw and breathed on me until I finally sat up.

"Tomorrow night is still a go?" she asked.

"Absolutely. I'm looking forward to it."

I was. I'd been mired in trying to figure out who killed Lewis Wallace for the past several days. It would be nice to think about something else other than that, or the fact that Ethan was leaving in less than two days.

As I drove up to Marcus's house it occurred to me that maybe I should stop poking around in Lewis Wallace's death. Maybe this time I should just leave everything to Marcus. He was good at his job, Derek had been cleared as a suspect and Ethan had never seriously been one. Maybe it was time to back off.

When I got to Marcus's house he was on the phone. He beckoned me inside. Just from his side of the conversation it seemed to involve a case. He ended the call and raked a hand back through his hair.

"Problem?" I asked.

"I'm sorry," he said. "That case of mine that's on trial? It's going to be going to the jury soon. The prosecutor needs to talk to me about a couple of things. I have to go."

"It's okay," I said. I stood on tiptoes and kissed him. "We can have lunch tomorrow and we're going out to Roma and Eddie's tomorrow night."

"Umm, yes to lunch and yes, I remembered about tomorrow night."

I kissed him again. "I'll meet you at Eric's at twelve. If anything changes, call me."

He promised he would and we walked out together. I headed home and he headed down the hill.

When I got home I found Ethan in the living room, watching a concert on his laptop with a bowl of popcorn and a cat on each side of him. It struck me that I wasn't going to be the only one who'd miss him. He pulled out one earbud. "Milo and Derek are bringing pizza. You want some?"

I shook my head. "Thanks, no. I'm just going to get a drink and then I have some stuff to do."

"Okay," he said. "Just come get a slice if you change your mind."

I made a cup of hot chocolate and headed upstairs. Hercules glanced in my direction but stayed where he was.

I took my hair out of the ponytail I'd worn to class and pulled on a pair of pajama pants and my favorite Boston College sweatshirt. The grocery list was still sitting on the nightstand. I picked it up.

Dwayne Parker. "Chunk," Wallace's ex-wife had called him. Was it even worth trying to find a phone number for the man? What could he tell me that would make a difference?

I thought about what Julie Kendall had told me, that Wallace had said that both he and Parker couldn't seem to get away from Saint Edwin's. Everything seemed to lead back to what really was just a minor cheating incident that had taken place at the school.

Finding a number for the man turned out to be easy. I just called the university's athletic office and they gave it to me without question.

I hesitated and then picked up my phone again.

Dwayne Parker had a big, booming voice that matched the mental image I had of a man whose nickname was Chunk. I explained who I was and asked Parker if Lewis Wallace had been in touch recently.

"Hell yeah," he said. "Three, maybe four weeks ago he called me outta nowhere. I hadn't talked to him in had to be ten years."

"So he just wanted to catch up?" I said.

"Nah, it was more than that. There was a kid that was in one of our classes—Lew and I were taking it for the second time because we hadn't really applied ourselves the first time." He laughed. "Anyways, this kid—he wasn't really a buddy, more a hanger-on if you know what I mean—his name was Carroll. Who the heck gives their kid a name like that anyway?"

I didn't think Parker was expecting an answer so I didn't comment.

"So Lew asked if I'd go see the guy's kid play, see if he was any good. I asked him why he wanted to do a favor for Christmas and his kid."

"Excuse me?" Had I heard him correctly? "Christmas?"

"Yeah. Lew always called the kid that because his name was Carroll. Get it? Christmas Carroll."

"I get it," I said.

Christmas. I had heard Wallace say that word when we were at The Brick that first night. I shook my head, trying to make all the pieces fall into place.

"So was he any good?" I asked.

"Yeah," Parker said. "I think we're gonna recruit him."

All roads led back to Saint Edwin's. "Do you remember Christmas's last name?"

He laughed. "Not a chance. I did a lot of partying back then. There's whole months I can't remember. Sorry. And the kid uses his mother's last name. Her and Christmas were never married."

"Do you happen to have any photos of . . . Christmas?"

"Probably." His voice boomed through the phone. It was a lot like talking to a big affable dog. "But I don't have a clue where they'd be."

I sighed. This wasn't going to work. "Thanks for talking to me," I said.

"You're welcome," he said. "I was sorry to hear about Lew, you know."

He was the first person to say that, I realized.

"Hey, you know, if you want to find a photo of Christmas you could try the school's website. They've got pictures going back for years for the football team. You should be able to find Christmas. He was one of the team's trainers."

I thanked him and said good night. Then I reached for my computer.

Saint Edwin's may have been a small school but they'd had eleven members of their football team play professionally in the last twenty-five years, I learned from their website. I scrolled through the photos looking for the years that Lewis Wallace and Chunk Parker had been at the college.

It was in the team photo from their second year that I found what I was looking for. I stared at the computer screen, not trusting what I was seeing. For a moment I forgot to breathe. My eyes were playing tricks on me. It was the only explanation.

I moved over closer to the lamp on the nightstand for more light. I had to be wrong. I *needed* to be wrong.

I wasn't wrong. Just like that, I knew who had killed Lewis

Wallace. The pieces fell into place like a puzzle I was looking at from another perspective.

Hercules had wandered into the room when I wasn't looking. He sat beside me now, eyes on the computer screen, and then cocked his head to one side.

"But how?" I said.

I looked at my old clock radio next to the lamp on the nightstand. I rarely used it because Hercules and his brother were pretty good about waking me long before I needed to get up, just the way Owen had that morning.

Time. That was it.

I sat there without moving, without speaking, sorting all the facts until they made a pattern. A pattern that said that I was right: There was only one possible killer.

I made one quick phone call. I only had one question to ask. Once I heard the answer I knew the how. And I was reasonably sure I also knew the why.

I ended the phone call and just sat there for a minute. Then I shut down the computer. I set it on the floor in front of the night table, precisely aligning it in the center between the two front legs of the stand. I picked up a bit of lint from the carpet. I buffed a fingerprint from the screen of my cell phone.

Hercules watched without comment. Finally, he climbed onto my lap and put one paw on my chest. I buried my face in his fur, and I cried.

chapter 16

After a minute or so I kissed the top of Hercules's head, got up and went to wash my face. Then I changed my pajama pants for jeans, gave my hair a brush and headed downstairs, Hercules beside me.

The guys were sitting at the kitchen table going over their set list, talking about which songs to keep and which to replace. There was a large pizza box on the table with a couple of slices left. Owen was sitting next to Ethan's chair.

"Hey, Kath, did you change your mind about the pizza?" Ethan asked, gesturing at the box. Milo and Derek both nodded hello.

I shook my head. "No." There was no way I could ever swallow past the lump in my throat.

I studied Ethan, hair wild as usual, gesturing with the pencil he was holding. He had such strong feelings about everything and for better or worse he brought that passion to everything he did. I remembered him as a baby and how quickly I came to love him and Sara with all that I had.

Owen walked around the table to me and I bent and picked him up, which gave me, somehow, a tiny shot of courage. He nuzzled my chin, Hercules leaned against my leg and I leaned against the counter.

Ethan looked across the table at Derek and then grinned at me. "Guess what?" he said. "Derek's going to join the band. I mean for good."

My stomach clutched.

Derek ran his fingers through his two-day-old beard. "I'm thinking I may have to get some dye for this," he said.

"Then you could pretend you're Liam's older brother instead of his dad," Milo joked.

"Derek, where is your son is going to school?" I asked.

He glanced over at me. "He hasn't decided yet. He's waiting to see how many offers he gets."

The lump at the back of my throat wouldn't go away. "But you're pulling for him to go to Saint Edwin's. It's kind of your alma mater."

"Derek didn't go to college, Kath," Ethan said without

even glancing up from the sheet of paper in front of him. "Remember?"

"Derek didn't *finish* college," I said.

Ethan frowned, finally looking up at me. "No. He didn't go in the first place, and what are you, the education police all of a sudden?"

"No one else would accept you, would they?" I said, keeping my eyes on Derek. If I looked at Ethan I'd start to cry again.

Ethan's dark eyes flashed. His expression was both angry and puzzled. "I don't know what you're talking about, Kathleen, but knock it off. Why don't you eat something? Maybe your blood sugar is low."

"How did you know?" Derek asked.

I knew those words were directed at me.

"I saw an old team photo of you standing in front of Lewis Wallace."

Ethan jumped to his feet, the chair scraping on the floor. "Derek didn't know that jerk, so will you please tell me what the hell is going on?"

I saw the realization dawn across Milo's face. "Stop talking," he said. He pushed his chair back and got to his feet as well. Ethan opened his mouth to say something and Milo put both hands on his chest and pushed him back into his seat. "Stop, just stop, okay?"

I think it was the first time I'd ever heard Milo raise his voice, even a little.

"Did you know he was going to be in town?" I asked Derek. I could see Ethan out of the corner of my eye, perched on the edge of his seat. I couldn't look directly at him because I was afraid I wouldn't be able to keep going.

"I found out he was maybe going to set up his new business here. When Ethan told me you lived here it just seemed like things were finally going to go my way."

"You wanted his help," I said. "You wanted your son to play football for the college that kicked you out."

"It was only fair," Derek said. "They screwed me over. I told Lewis we needed to talk in person. I told him we'd be here. He agreed to meet me but said we had to keep the fact that we knew each other quiet. He didn't want anyone to find out about the whole cheating thing. He had something going that could be ruined for him. I wanted him to put in a good word for Liam. After all, he owed me." He was holding a pencil in his right hand, turning it slowly between his thumb and index finger.

"All those years ago he paid you to take the blame for stealing those test answers." I didn't say the words as a question because I already knew the answer.

"He said all they'd do was put me on academic probation. They kicked me out!" Anger flashed in his eyes. He swallowed hard a couple of times.

From the corner of my eye I could see Ethan staring up at the ceiling as if somehow there were answers up there. He looked in my direction, anger etched in the lines on his face.

"Liam has talent," Derek said. His eyes were glued to my face. It was like we were the only two people in the room. "I knew all he needed was to get into a good college program. I knew Lewis still had connections with the football program at Saint Edwin's. A few weeks ago I finally got in touch with him. He kept saying he'd do something but nothing happened. Finally, that night he admitted he couldn't write the letter. He said it would look suspicious if he spoke up for the kid of the guy who got kicked out for doing what *he'd* originally been accused of. He said he could help in other ways. He offered me money. He tried to buy me off again!"

Ethan was so jumpy I thought he was going to come out of his skin. "Kathleen, tell me what the hell is going on," he all but shouted at me.

Derek finally shifted his attention away from me. He looked at Ethan. "It's been good working with you guys. It's been better than good, but we don't exactly live in the same worlds."

"What is that supposed to mean?" Milo asked.

"It means I've had to fight for every damn thing I've ever gotten. No one's ever given me a break."

"So that makes it okay to kill somebody?"

Derek shook his head and his mouth twisted to one side. "You saw the kind of man Lewis Wallace was."

Milo was already shaking his head. "That doesn't make it right."

Ethan jumped out of his chair. It fell backward, hitting the floor. "Kathleen, this is crazy," he shouted. His hands were everywhere. "You know Derek didn't kill anyone. Some guy you know gave him an alibi."

Derek looked up at me. "I don't understand that part. When Marcus came and said someone had given me an alibi, I couldn't figure it out. Who did he see?"

"He saw you," I said. My hands were shaking. "He just got the time wrong. Ian Queen's battery was dead on his phone. His old truck didn't have a clock—or a working radio. When he walked into his mother's house he looked at the clock for the time. The thing is, Patricia is one of those nitpicky people. It was the night we switched to daylight savings time. Right after supper she changed every clock in her house. When Ian looked at the time—"

"—it was wrong," Derek finished.

"Yes."

He sighed. "I was going to confess. I swear to you that I was and then Marcus walked in and said some guy had given me an alibi and I thought maybe it was some way that the universe was evening things up and I just . . . I just kept my mouth shut."

I nodded. I could understand that.

Derek shrugged. "You know, the funny thing is, I didn't even know where Lewis was. Then I got one of those stupid alumni newsletters they sent out. They must have gotten my address from my mother. It had this section where they say what people are doing now."

"And you found out that Wallace was doing pretty well."

"Yeah. He cheated and they were writing about him like he was some big deal. At first, I was just going to out him, tell the truth. But I figured, who was going to believe me over him? So I thought, why not get something for myself, for my kid?"

"That night at the bar, he called you Christmas."

He nodded. "He gave me that stupid nickname the first time we met. Even though we agreed we weren't going to let on we knew each other he said it, out of habit, he claimed."

Owen shifted in my arms and I stroked his soft gray fur. "How did you know Wallace was at the hotel and how did you know where the meeting room was?" I asked.

"It was the nicest hotel in town. Where else would he stay? As for the meeting room, Ethan had sent me a text about getting the muffins for your friend Maggie and putting them in the meeting room so you wouldn't find out."

I heard Ethan make a strangled oath.

"He said he'd just walked through the lobby and no one had stopped him. I knew Lewis had always had problems getting to sleep and would probably be up. I was going to go up to his room but there he was, wandering around the hallways. I pulled him into the meeting room to talk, popped the lock the same way Milo had shown me once."

He looked at Milo. "Sorry, man," he said in a voice barely above a whisper.

I set Owen on the floor, giving Hercules a quick scratch on

the head as I straightened up. I folded my arms across my chest. The room suddenly seemed colder. Or maybe it was just me.

"He wouldn't help me," Derek said in a voice laced with bitterness. "I told him I'd tell everyone that he paid me to lie and say I stole those test answers. He said no one would believe me."

It occurred to me that was probably true.

"He said he'd help me some other way but he couldn't let the truth come out, not now. I knew what that meant. I wasn't taking another payoff. He grabbed one of those muffins and . . . I didn't stop him. In fact, I smashed it into his fat mouth. I didn't mean to kill him."

"You took his EpiPen away from him."

"He dropped it on the floor." Derek looked away.

"You kicked it across the room," I said.

"Not to kill him!"

"Well what did you think was going to happen?" Milo asked.

Derek looked from me to Milo. "He owed me. Don't you get it? I just wanted what he owed me."

"Do you remember Dwayne Parker?" I asked.

Derek frowned. "Dwayne? Wait a sec, you mean Chunk?"

I nodded. "He works at Saint Edwin's. Wallace called him. Asked him to go see your son play."

He shook his head. "I don't understand."

"Wallace said he was going to help you and he did. Saint

Edwin's is probably going to offer Liam a scholarship. You got what you wanted, what you seem to think you were owed. You didn't need to kill him."

The door opened then and Marcus stepped into the kitchen. I'd called him before I'd come downstairs. He started to read Derek his rights. I walked into the living room. I knew what was coming and I didn't want to watch that part.

chapter 17

Marcus left with Derek, and Ethan walked out of the house without saying a word. Milo gave my shoulder a squeeze. "I'll go after him," he said.

I curled up on one of the chairs with Owen and Hercules together on my lap until Roma walked in and wrapped her arms around me.

We were at the table talking over cups of tea, with Hercules on my lap and Owen at my feet checking out the crackers Roma had given him, when Ethan walked in. He came to a skidding stop just inside the kitchen door.

I got to my feet, setting Hercules on the seat of the chair. I went to my little brother, wrapping my arms around him just the way Roma had done with me.

"I'm sorry for running off," he said against my shoulder.

"It's okay," I said, hugging him even harder.

Ethan and Milo joined us at the table. Milo extended his hand to Roma and said, "Milo."

She took it, smiling. "Roma."

Ethan had questions and I tried to answer them without drowning him in information.

"I can't believe it," he said, raking both hands back through his hair. "I know Derek could be self-absorbed sometimes and intense, but I can't believe he'd kill someone."

I nodded. "I know. And I'm sorry this happened."

"Are you kidding?" Ethan asked. "Derek was here because of me. If anyone's at fault, it's me."

"That's crazy," I said. "None of this is your fault. You're not to blame for any of this."

Ethan reached across the table and grabbed my hand. "Then you're not, either," he said.

The get-together at Roma's was canceled. I spent Friday evening with Ethan, just the two of us.

"You guys need some alone time," Milo had said.

The two of them left the next morning to pick up Devon. "I think the true-love thing may be fading," Milo said with a laugh. I stood next to the van and hugged my brother hard.

"I love you," he said, giving me an equally fierce squeeze.

"I love you, too, brat," I said.

He grinned as he let me go. "Tell Maggie I said good-bye."

"I will," I promised. I fixed his hair. "Stay out of trouble."

They pulled out of the driveway and I waved until I couldn't see the van anymore.

The library closed at one o'clock on Thursday to get ready for the grand opening of the quilt show. I went home to change and grab a quick bite and when I stepped back inside at quarter after six it struck me that the building had never looked so full of color and life. The quilts were everywhere I looked. Big ones. Small ones. Rectangular, square and round. They were more than fabric, batting and thread. They were art; beautiful, detailed pieces of art.

Oren was standing by the circulation desk looking up at one of Patricia's vintage quilts suspended from the ceiling. He was wearing a charcoal-gray suit with a white shirt and blue striped tie. He looked very nice, and a little uncomfortable. I walked over to join him.

"Hello, Kathleen," he said.

I smiled at him. "Hello, Oren. You've outdone yourself."

He smiled back at me. "Thank you, but the credit should go to Patricia and the other quilters."

"They've done spectacular work and I've already told them that, but their efforts wouldn't be getting the audience they deserve if you hadn't found a way to safely display everything. So you get some of the credit, too."

Oren gestured at the incredibly detailed crazy quilt he'd been studying. "Did you know that one is over a hundred years old? My father and mother hadn't been born when it was made."

The tiny pieces of fabric that made up the quilt were faded to soft muted versions of their original colors, but they were still beautiful. "I'm amazed to think that every bit of work was done by hand," I said.

"I'm happy people still care about that kind of thing," Oren said.

I turned in a slow circle, taking in the quilts over my head. Like Oren, I was happy that people still appreciated the time and skill that had gone into making them.

Abigail was over in our computer space. Two of the computers had temporarily been moved to the magazine section. The others were upstairs for the three days of the show. Abigail beckoned me over.

I touched Oren on the arm. "I'll talk to you later," I said.

He nodded.

Abigail had set out the trays of cookies. On a third table there was a printed listing of all the quilts in the show with a brief description of each piece and of the people who had worked on it. "How does everything look?" she asked.

"Beautiful," I said. "And so do you."

She was wearing a deep kelly green dress with black tights and black ankle boots.

"Thank you," she said with a smile. "So do you."

I was wearing my favorite cobalt-blue sweater dress and a pair of completely-impractical-for-Mayville-Heights-in-the-winter spike-heeled black suede boots.

"There's just something about having all this color around in the middle of winter that made me want to put on something bright," I said.

Abigail nodded. "Me too."

I glanced at my watch. "I'm going to do one last walk-around."

Abigail grinned at me. "We're ready, Kathleen." She held out both hands. "Everything looks fantastic. Harry even cleaned the windows. We have cookies."

I leaned my head to one side and silently looked at her. After a moment she shook her head. "I'll come with you," she said. She knew me well.

We opened the door to the show precisely at seven o'clock. There was a line of people waiting outside to come in. I welcomed everyone and Patricia shared a little about the quilters and their history. Then we turned everyone loose to look.

I walked around saying hello to people, answering questions where I could and deferring to Patricia and her quilters when I couldn't. They were all wearing patchwork tags with their names—Patricia's idea—which made them easy to find.

I was standing at the bottom of the stairs when Eric touched me on the shoulder. "This is incredible." He gestured with one hand. "I've never seen so many people here."

"I don't think we've ever had so many people in the building all at once," I said. I pointed in the general direction of the computer space. "Your cookies are a hit. Thank you again for sharing the recipe."

"You're welcome," he said. "I'm honored to be a tiny part of all of this." He leaned in. "Could I make a bit of a confession?"

I nodded. Was he going to tell me he'd stolen the recipe from Martha Stewart?

That wasn't it. "I, uh, had a pretty stereotypical view of quilting as something that was done by white-haired little old ladies who made patchwork square coverlets for their grandbabies' beds."

He glanced over at Ella King with her blue-streaked hair courtesy of Ruby, talking about her art quilt, a portrait of her daughter Taylor.

"I think you may need to revise that definition a bit," I said, giving him a little nudge with my shoulder.

By eight o'clock the workshops were filled and there was a waiting list for all of them. Patricia was talking to Ruby about doing something in conjunction with the artists' co-op. Melanie was fielding questions from tourists about things to do and see in the area. Maggie and Roma joined me to share that they had snagged the last seats in the beginner's quilting workshop.

"I think quilting has so much potential for my collage work," Maggie said.

Roma smiled. "I think the whole process of sewing by hand feels almost like meditation."

Marcus came up behind me and put an arm around my waist. "Congratulations," he said. "You've done an incredible job. But then, you always do."

I smiled up at him. "Did it occur to you that you might be a little biased?"

"Not in the slightest." He kissed the top of my head. "Saturday night we're going to celebrate, just the two of us."

I nodded. *And I'm finally going to tell you the truth,* I added silently.

Marcus brought shrimp pasta from Eric's for supper on Saturday night. After we'd eaten and the dishes were finished I sat down across from him at the table. "I need to talk to you about something," I said.

"Sure," he said, curiosity in his blue eyes. "What is it?"

"What happened with Derek really brought home to me the danger of secrets. I'm sorry I've kept this secret for so long." I tucked a strand of hair behind my ear. I couldn't seem to keep my hands still. "It's not that I didn't—don't—trust you, it's just that for so long it didn't seem like we were going to be a couple and then when we were I just didn't know how to tell you and I kept putting it off and . . ." I realized I was babbling.

"Just tell me what's wrong."

My hands were suddenly sweaty and I wiped them on my

jeans. "Do you remember the other day when we were in the porch and you turned around and Owen was just suddenly there?"

He nodded. "Yes."

"You said you didn't see him when you came in."

He nodded again.

"You were right. You didn't see him because you couldn't."

Marcus smiled. "Is this your way of telling me you think I need glasses?"

I cleared my throat. "No, that's not it. You couldn't see Owen because he was invisible."

He frowned. "You're not making sense."

"I know it sounds crazy," I said, and it did, just listening to myself say the words out loud. "Owen can disappear. And Micah, too. That's the reason you didn't see her until she suddenly appeared in the car out in the driveway."

I could see the concern in his eyes, like clouds filling a blue sky.

"Kathleen, you've had a very stressful few days," he began. "You're tired and overloaded."

I shook my head vigorously. "This is not stress and I'm not crazy. Owen can disappear and Hercules can walk through walls." I picked up Owen and set him on the empty chair next to Marcus. "Disappear," I said.

The cat blinked at me and took a couple of passes at his face with one paw. He was enjoying this.

Marcus grabbed my hand. "I'm going to call Roma."

I yanked my hand back. "Marcus, I'm not crazy and I don't need Roma. She's an animal doctor for heaven's sake, and I don't need a doctor, period."

"I'm sorry," he said. "I'm just worried about you." There were lines pulling at his eyes and mouth.

I looked down at Hercules, who had wandered in from the living room. "Go out to the porch," I said.

"Merow," he said, and it seemed to me there was a question in the sound.

"Please."

He turned and walked toward the door.

Marcus made a move to go to open it but I grabbed his arm. Hercules stopped at the closed door, looked over his shoulder at me and then with a slight shimmer walked through it.

Marcus was frozen in place. Then slowly he turned to look at me. "It's some kind of trick," he said.

I shook my head.

"There's some kind of panel in the door."

"You know that's not true."

I let go of his arm and he ran his hands through his hair. "This doesn't make sense."

"I think it has something to do with Wisteria Hill."

"Why?"

I made a helpless gesture with one hand. "I don't know, but all three cats came from there."

Owen had been watching everything. I turned back to him. "Owen, please. Show Marcus."

The cat almost seemed to shrug and then he winked out of sight. The color drained from Marcus's face. "I'm not seeing this," he said.

"That's how I felt the first time. I didn't think I'd ever get used to it but I did."

Owen reappeared.

Marcus didn't seem to know what to do with his hands. "You think Micah can do all this?"

"She can disappear like Owen. As far as I know she can't walk through walls like Hercules."

"When did you figure this out?" he asked.

"She disappeared right in front of me one day."

His eyes widened. "Wait a minute, you've known the entire time I've had Micah, then."

"Not at first, but I have known for a while." I jammed my hands in my pockets.

"How long have you known about Hercules and Owen?"

I looked away. "I figured it out when the work was being done at the library."

He did the math. "More than three years?"

"Yes. But we weren't together then. We weren't together for a long time. I had to keep it secret. If anyone finds out what they can do they'll be taken to a lab and their brains will be"—my voice broke—"dissected. They'll be a science experiment."

"So the time Hercules stowed away in that guy's car . . . ?"

"He walked through the back window."

"Do you know how many laws of physics this violates?" Marcus asked. He looked shell-shocked.

"Well . . . in the case of Owen disappearing, possibly none. It may be that somehow something in his cells allows light waves to bend around him. He doesn't dematerialize. You just can't see him. As for Hercules, matter can pass through other matter. Neutrinos are passing through us right now." I'd done a lot of research trying to come up with an explanation for the boys' abilities.

"You should have told me."

"I know. I kept putting it off and it just got harder. I'm sorry. I know I keep saying that but I am."

Marcus looked at Owen. He looked over at the door that Hercules had disappeared through. He took a step backward.

"I, uh, I need some air," he said. He grabbed his jacket and was gone.

He was gone.

I swallowed hard. "I lied to him," I said to Owen. "I lied to him, so what did I expect?"

I straightened the chairs around the table. I got the coffee-pot ready for morning and took muffins from the freezer.

I gave Owen two stinky crackers just because.

He looked in the direction of the porch and meowed.

"I'll take a couple out to your brother," I said.

Hercules wasn't in the porch. He'd gone outside where it was cold and dark and wet? I opened the back door.

Hercules was perched on the wide arm of the wooden

Adirondack chair that I had dragged out during our late-February warm spell—more for him than for me. Marcus was sitting in the chair.

He was still here.

He hadn't gone anywhere.

I stood in the open doorway for a moment, not sure what to do.

"I love you," he said. He didn't move and he didn't look in my direction.

"I love you, too," I said. Then I closed the door and went back inside.